AN HEIR
MADE IN THE
MARRIAGE BED

AN HEIR
MADE IN THE
MARRIAGE BED

BY

ANNE MATHER

First published in Great Britain 2017
By Mills & Boon, an imprint of HarperCollins*Publishers*
1 London Bridge Street, London, SE1 9GF

Large Print edition 2017

© 2017 Anne Mather

ISBN: 978-0-263-07164-1

Printed and bound in Great Britain
by CPI Group (UK) Ltd, Croydon, CR0 4YY

To my wonderful family, Fred, Kate, Nick, Lyn, Abi and Ben, and not forgetting Dolly.

What would I do without you?

CHAPTER ONE

THE LATE AFTERNOON sun was still too hot.

Matt Novak shifted impatiently on the cushioned recliner his mother had had one of the maids place in the shaded area of the patio. The khaki shorts he was wearing with a black tee shirt were damp with perspiration. But he intended to go to the gym later. He was sick and tired of doing nothing at all.

Ahead of him, sunlight was dazzling on the waters of the canal that lapped against the sea wall. Even the dark sunglasses he was wearing couldn't entirely protect his eyes from the glare of the bay beyond.

There was a banyan tree beside the patio, its gnarled branches almost invisible beneath trailing blossoms of flowering vines. His father's sailing dinghy was tied to the dock, rocking gently at its mooring. He could smell the dampness of the vegetation growing out of the waterway and the unmistakeable scent of the sea.

It was all very beautiful and very peaceful, but Matt had had enough of being treated like an invalid. To begin with, it had been quite pleasant to be waited on hand and foot, but now his mother was beginning to get on his nerves. She made no attempt to hide her disapproval when he went and bench-pressed his own weight in the gym. She really didn't want to accept that he was feeling fine.

As witness her reluctance to let him use a computer.

His own laptop and phone had been stolen while he was in the hospital in Caracas, and to begin with he couldn't have cared less. The tropical fever that had struck him down during his trip to Venezuela had been very unpleasant, and he'd needed all his strength to defeat it. But his mother wouldn't accept that he was over that now, and she was doing everything in her power to keep him here in Coral Gables.

The only fly in her ointment was that his father had abandoned his retirement and taken over the New York office of Novak Oil Exploration and Shipping again. Matt's job until three months ago.

He scowled. Not that he objected to that. He'd already decided that spending the rest of his life in a boardroom wasn't for him. Now he had to convince his parents of the fact.

However that wasn't all that was bugging him at this moment. Despite the many emails he'd asked his mother to send to his estranged wife who lived in London, Joanna hadn't responded to any of them.

Yes, she was probably still mad at him. He got that. But didn't she care now if he lived or died? It seemed not, and, although he had replaced his iPhone, she'd changed her number after their separation.

He could have rung the gallery where she was working, but he had no desire to speak to David Bellamy. He had more pride than to admit he didn't have his wife's new number. But he was planning to leave for London at the end of the week. The sooner he could speak to her in person, the better.

The sound of a car's engine broke the silence.

Matt stiffened, wondering who was visiting his mother today. Then he remembered. His sister, Sophie, who was staying with them at the moment, had gone into Miami to see one of her friends off at the airport. He thought the engine was that of his mother's little Mazda, but, at the sound of more than one pair of footsteps coming along the paved pathway from the front of the house, he wondered who the hell Sophie had brought back with her.

Not another woman for him to admire, he hoped. He'd had his fill of his mother's attempts to interest him in some well-connected girl. He and Joanna might be having their problems, but they were still married and he firmly believed they'd eventually work their issues out.

But it wasn't a friend of Sophie's. Well, only indirectly.

The young woman following his sister was far more familiar to him. Tall and slim, yet with a curvaceous figure, shown to effect in an open-necked silk shirt and a swirly skirt that ended just above her knees, she looked stunning. A sexy riot of sun-streaked hair curled about her shoulders, and she met his startled gaze with wary violet eyes.

The last time he'd seen his estranged wife had been at her father's funeral nine months ago. Though on that occasion she hadn't known he was there. Before that, it had been when she'd walked out of their London apartment. She'd sworn then she never wanted to see him again, and yet here she was.

Halleluiah!

Sophie looked anxious, he thought. 'Look who

I found at the airport,' she exclaimed, trying for a cheerful tone, and Matt got instantly to his feet.

For her part, Joanna was on edge. She hadn't wanted to come here, to Matt's parents' house. Not like this. She needed to speak to her husband, of course she did, but she'd booked herself a room for the night at a hotel on Miami Beach and she'd been hoping to invite Matt to join her for dinner that evening. Turning up here, unannounced, had not been her intention.

Until Sophie had informed her that Matt had been seriously ill.

When she'd boarded the flight from New York to Miami that morning, she hadn't really known if she'd find her husband here. He wasn't in London, and she'd discovered he wasn't at the New York office either, so she'd known he could be anywhere.

The Novak Corporation or NovCo, as it appeared on the stock exchange, had offices all over the world. But Matt tended to work in one of two places and, after flying to New York and learning that only the elder Mr Novak was available, she'd felt compelled to try here.

Of course, she'd wondered why Matt's father should be in charge. Oliver Novak had retired to Florida a couple of years ago, and Joanna was sure he wouldn't have returned to work unless something was wrong. But even then, it hadn't occurred to her that Matt might be involved.

She could have asked to speak to Oliver, she supposed. That would have been the sensible thing to do. But, much as she liked Matt's father, she was loath to involve him in what was actually a personal affair. This was something she needed to speak to her husband about herself.

She'd decided to come to Florida as a last resort. It didn't necessarily follow that if Oliver Novak was in New York, his son was in Miami, but it was worth a try. Maybe Matt wasn't reading his emails, which she found hard to believe. Or maybe he was simply ignoring her demands.

She wasn't looking forward to seeing his mother again. Adrienne Novak had never liked her. Joanna was sure she'd have been delighted when she and Matt separated. She'd never regarded Joanna as good enough for her son, and had lost no opportunity to create trouble for them.

It had been particularly painful for Joanna when she and Matt had been trying for a baby. Despite consulting fertility calendars and temperature gauges, Joanna hadn't fallen pregnant, and Adrienne had implied that, as the Novaks' only

son, Matt naturally wanted an heir. And if not
with her…

Adrienne hadn't finished the sentence, but Joanna had known exactly what she meant. Her
mother-in-law had taken every opportunity to
turn the knife.

It was totally by chance that Joanna had run
into Matt's sister at the airport. Sophie had been
there to say goodbye to a friend from California,
and she'd been delighted to see her sister-in-law.

She and Joanna had been good friends in the
days when they had lived in New York. Sophie
was older than Matt, but nothing at all like her
mother. She'd sympathised with Joanna's disappointment at not having a baby, even though her
own marriage, engineered by her mother, was
heading for the rocks.

Sophie, learning that Joanna was here to see
Matt, had suggested that she should come back
to the house with her. And when Joanna had demurred, explaining that she'd planned to stay at a
hotel for tonight, Sophie had said something that
had totally changed her mind.

'Matt's virtually recovered now and he'll be so
glad to see you,' she'd chattered on guilelessly.
'You know what my mother's like. Even though

Matt's got over the infection, she's hoping to keep him at home for a few more days at least.'

Not knowing what Sophie was talking about, Joanna had been shocked to learn that her husband was recovering from some tropical illness he'd picked up in South America. It explained why their father was running the company in his absence, but she wished someone had let her know.

Matt wouldn't want her to stay at a hotel, Sophie had insisted, although Joanna had seen the curiosity in her sister-in-law's eyes. Which begged the question, what had Matt told his parents about their break-up? Surely, he'd explained to his family why Joanna was trying to contact him now?

It seemed not.

Whatever, Joanna had known she wouldn't be welcome at the house in Coral Gables whether Matt was there or not. Yet if Matt's mother knew why she'd been trying to get in touch with her son, why hadn't she told him? Bearing in mind the length of their separation, Joanna was surprised she hadn't persuaded her son to apply for a divorce himself.

Sophie, of course, had jumped to her own conclusions. She'd assumed her sister-in-law was here to heal the breach. 'I know you and Matt have had your problems,' she'd said, aware that Joanna and her brother had been living apart for the past eleven months. 'But I'm sure you've both had time to realise you need one another. Matt's been pretty down ever since he came back from Venezuela.'

Which would be the result of the infection he'd picked up, Joanna had reminded herself firmly. It was unlikely his depression had anything to do with her. But Sophie had always been her friend and she'd been loath to upset her. And perhaps the sooner the confrontation was over—if there was to be a confrontation—the better.

Matt's eyes were hidden behind dark glasses, and, despite her nerves, Joanna couldn't help noticing that he had lost weight. Yet, at thirty-eight, he would still draw women's eyes wherever he went, she conceded bitterly. She'd always thought he was the sexiest man she'd ever known.

But she wasn't here to conduct a one-woman lust-fest, she thought irritably. Looking at him now, she felt sure the emails she'd sent must have reached him. Surely, he hadn't been so ill that he couldn't read his mail?

Despite his loss of weight, he looked reasonably fit. And just as disturbingly attractive as before. There was a brooding sensuality about his dark countenance that had always caused a pleasurable buzz inside her. And despite everything that had gone before, she was unhappily aware that that hadn't changed.

Some people might say that his eyes were too deep-set or his mouth too thin, but she knew better. Matt's looks were too sensual to be ignored. Which was why she'd sent the emails in the first place; why she'd hoped he wouldn't contest her request for a divorce. She'd fought against having to see him again. She'd known how vulnerable she still was where he was concerned.

It was infuriating, but she couldn't deny the way her breathing hitched when he came towards her. *Don't touch me,* she thought, panicking, and felt a totally ridiculous urge to flee.

'Jo,' he said, pulling off his sunglasses, his deep voice scraping like sandpaper over her tortured nerves. 'How good of you to come.'

Was that sarcasm in his voice? Joanna couldn't be sure, but when he held out a hand to her, she pretended not to see it. She didn't want him to detect the crazy tattoo of her heart or the heat that swept up her throat from her chest at his nearness. But she was unhappily aware that the hollow between her breasts revealed a betraying trace of moisture to his narrow-eyed gaze.

'Sophie says you've been ill,' she said quickly, sensing his appraisal and wishing she hadn't unfastened her shirt on the trip from the airport. The vest below the shirt was adequate, but hardly modest. 'I'm sorry. Are you feeling better now?'

Matt's hand dropped to his side and he regarded her through puzzled eyes. His dark lashes narrowed his gaze, but she sensed she'd said—and probably done—the wrong thing. Didn't he know that no one had thought to inform her of his state of health?

'I'm surprised you took so long to get here,' he responded, unknowingly answering her question. And Sophie, sensing that all was not as it should be, broke in.

'I found Joanna at the airport,' she exclaimed, evidently trying to divert the conversation. 'She'd just flown in from New York this morning. She was planning to book into a hotel, but I persuaded her to come with me instead.'

'Really?' said Matt, and from his tone Joanna sensed he definitely wasn't pleased. His eyes impaled her. 'Why were you planning on staying at a hotel?'

'I thought it was wise.' Joanna tried to sound casual. 'After all, this is your parents' house and I hadn't warned anyone I was coming.'

'Did you feel you had to?'

'Obviously,' she said, not really understanding where this was going.

'But you got the emails my mother sent you, I assume,' said Matt impatiently. 'I have to admit, I'd expected a more—what shall I say? —sympathetic response?'

Which was when Sophie evidently decided to leave them to it. With a rueful wave of her hand, and a 'See you later', she slipped away into the house.

But as far as Joanna was concerned, the older girl's departure only heightened the tension between them and she took an involuntary step backwards. What emails was he talking about? Evidently not her own.

Shaking her head, she went on, 'Believe it or not, when I flew down from New York, I knew nothing about your illness. If I had, I'd have got in touch with you sooner. When I found out you weren't at the New York office, I could only guess where you might be.'

'Didn't my father tell you?' Matt asked impatiently, and then realised that if Oliver had seen Joanna—or spoken to her, for that matter—he'd have let his son know.

'I didn't speak to your father,' said Joanna uncomfortably. 'I wanted to speak to you.'

'Am I to understand that you've had no word from me?'

'Yes.' Joanna squared her shoulders. 'Why would I lie?'

'Why indeed?'

Joanna was indignant. 'If you'd bothered to read any of my messages, you'd know why I'm here.'

'*Your* messages?' Matt looked bemused and Joanna felt a sense of disbelief.

'This is ridiculous,' she exclaimed. 'We're talking at cross purposes here. I'm talking about the half-dozen or so emails I've sent you in the past few weeks.' She steeled herself to meet his gaze. 'I can't believe you haven't read any of them.'

'I haven't.' Matt returned her stare. 'First of all, I've been in hospital in both Caracas and Miami. And afterwards, I let my mother deal with any correspondence.'

Oh, why am I not surprised? thought Joanna bitterly, as comprehension dawned. What a golden opportunity for Adrienne to drive another wedge between them this had been.

If there hadn't been one there already, she appended bitterly.

'That's why my father's in New York.' Matt lifted his shoulders in a dismissive gesture. 'As soon as he realised I'd need some time to convalesce, he insisted on taking over. I suspect retirement was getting boring. Whatever, he couldn't wait to get on the plane.'

Taking over was something the Novaks were very familiar with, Joanna thought grimly. But when Oliver Novak had had a mild stroke two years ago, his doctors had advised him to give up his job as CEO of NovCo.

That was when Matt had taken over, and because Joanna hadn't wanted to leave her father, who'd just been diagnosed with lung cancer, Matt had agreed that he should divide his time between the New York hub and the London affiliate.

A double-edged sword, Joanna admitted now. Her and Matt's relationship had already been strained by their inability to conceive, and her unwillingness to discuss her feelings with him. It hadn't helped at all to hear about Matt wining and dining male and female investors, even though that had always been part of his job.

It had never bothered her before, she conceded. In those days, she'd believed Matt loved her, and she'd trusted him implicitly. But being unable to conceive had made her vulnerable, in ways she'd never considered before.

'I had no idea what was going on,' she declared now, looping the strap of her bag over her shoulder and straightening her spine to face him. 'I'm not without feelings, you know.'

But she suspected she now knew what had happened to the messages she'd sent Matt. If they'd passed through his mother's hands, Adrienne must have read them. But that didn't really explain why she hadn't passed them on.

Nevertheless, her reasons for being here hadn't changed. She wanted a divorce. It was as simple and as complicated as that. Simple, because all Matt had to do was agree not to contest it; and complicated, because when her father sold his small company to the Novak Corporation, Matt had made her a shareholder in NovCo.

Not that she wanted any part of the organisation now. But the legal aspects of the situation would have to be gone through. She had hoped that after this interview Matt might come to London, which would have made things easier. But she was here now and she had to accept the situation as it was.

She should have taken David Bellamy's advice, she thought ruefully. Her boss at the art gallery, where she'd been working when she met Matt and where she was working again now, had warned her she should leave any communication between them to a solicitor. David had never liked Matt. He had been of the opinion that a man like Matthew

Novak was used to women falling at his feet, and he'd been convinced their marriage wouldn't last.

And it hadn't.

'You know what he's like,' David had said on more than one occasion. 'He believes he can twist you round his little finger. And if he thinks I'm involved in your decision, he's bound to be suspicious. Do you really want to give him the chance to change your mind?'

'Matt couldn't do that,' she'd retorted at once, the distance between them convincing her she was right.

And she was right, she silently insisted. She had only to think of her father, and the torment he must have suffered during his last illness, to know there was no going back.

Of course, that was months ago now, and her father was dead. But the bitterness she'd felt towards Matt had never gone away. She'd even convinced herself that the love they'd shared had been only a mirage. She was an independent woman these days and she wanted to keep it that way.

Ergo, the divorce.

Even so, she hadn't been prepared for learning that Matt had been ill. When Sophie had first told her what had been going on, her reaction had made a mockery of everything she'd claimed.

She'd truly believed she was immune to Matt's dark attraction; that she'd be able to look at him and speak to him without feeling the pull of his sensuality.

But once again, she'd been wrong...

CHAPTER TWO

YET WHAT DID that mean? That she was having second thoughts? But no, Joanna assured herself severely. She was merely reacting to the sexuality of the man, not to any lingering emotions she might feel.

Matt was regarding her with brooding eyes. Clearly, he was as bemused by the situation as she was. But he evidently had his own agenda, and, gesturing towards the chairs, he said, 'Why don't you sit down? I'll order some refreshments. If you didn't come to find out if I was still alive, why are you here?'

Joanna hesitated. Did she really want to behave as if this were just a social visit? Yet what else could she do in the present circumstances?

So, 'All right,' she said offhandedly and a snap of Matt's fingers brought one of the household staff to the patio.

He ordered both coffee and a jug of iced tea,

and then suggested that Joanna should take the lounger beside his own.

There were several chairs set in the shade of a striped awning and, resigning herself to the situation, Joanna took the one he indicated. But she couldn't help stiffening when Matt seated himself beside her, lowering the footrest and turning his chair sideways so that his bare knees were only inches from her own.

They were alone, and Joanna put down her handbag and smoothed her hair back from her face. It had been tumbled on the ride from the airport, and she wished she'd had time to use a comb. Sophie's car was a convertible, and, endeavouring a compromise, Joanna looped several errant strands behind her ears.

Matt, watching her, couldn't help noticing how silky her hair was and recalling how soft her skin used to feel beneath his hands. It had been too long since they'd been together and he was impatient to tell her that, whatever had gone before, he was sorry they'd been living apart.

But would she be any more inclined to hear it now than she had before?

Meanwhile, Joanna was wishing she hadn't run into Sophie at the airport. A phone call to the

Novaks' house would have surely elicited the information that Matt had been ill and she might well have waited until tomorrow before contacting him. She was not without feelings, but if she'd been able to invite Matt to the hotel, she would have felt a little more in control.

'So…' Matt regarded her enquiringly, arching a dark brow. 'Do I take it you have not forgiven me?'

Joanna pressed her lips together. His words were so unexpected. 'Did you think I would?'

'It has been nine months since your father died,' declared Matt quietly. 'I regret that whole incident, but it wasn't my fault.'

Joanna stared at him. 'Yes, so you said,' she declared coolly. 'Nevertheless, my father trusted you.'

'And I trusted him,' he said harshly, unable to prevent himself, 'which shows what a fool I was. Angus Carlyle trusted no one. Even your mother realised that.'

'Leave my mother out of this,' exclaimed Joanna tersely. 'She was hardly a role model. She had an affair with another man.'

'Not while she was married to your father. Glenys met Lionel Avery after she'd asked for a divorce,' declared Matt flatly. 'I hope you haven't continued to hold that against her.'

'My relationship with my mother is no concern of yours.'

'No.' Matt conceded the fact. 'But Angus was a jealous man, Jo. He resented the fact that she was happy. He resented our marriage, as well.'

'That's not true!'

'Of course, it's true. You were his little girl. He wanted to keep you that way. I'm surprised he let you work at Bellamy's gallery. He can't have known the guy was in love with you, too.'

Joanna's jaw dropped. 'That's ridiculous! David doesn't love me.'

Matt shrugged and expelled a weary breath. Reaching for her hand, he ran his fingers sensuously over her knuckles. 'Let's not talk about Bellamy or your father, Jo. The past is the past. I prefer to think about the future.'

Joanna had felt as if she were frozen until he touched her, but now she snatched her hand away. 'We have no future,' she said abruptly. 'You have to know that.'

Matt's expression darkened once again. 'I know nothing of the kind,' he replied, though there was a trace of bitterness in his tone now. 'Are you going to let your father's lies ruin your whole life?'

'My father didn't lie to me,' she declared stiffly. 'He told me the truth.'

'His truth.' Matt gazed at her with frustrated eyes. 'I love you, Jo. Tell me what I can do to make things right.'

It was an actual effort, but Joanna dragged her eyes away from his. 'I haven't come here to try and mend our differences.'

Matt's lips twisted. 'I had guessed that.'

'So, you must have realised—'

But she didn't get to finish her sentence. Before she could blurt out that the only reason she was here was because she wanted a divorce, the man who had taken Matt's order for refreshments returned.

And he wasn't alone. An older woman, dressed in grey silk lounging pants and a matching grey smock, emerged from the villa behind them.

'Matt,' she began, her drawling voice revealing her discontent. 'What is this Aaron tells me about you having a visitor? Someone Sophie brought back from the airport?'

And then, she saw Joanna, and her lips tightened angrily.

'My God,' she exclaimed, involuntarily Joanna was sure.

'I—what are you doing here?'

* * *

A couple of hours later, Joanna was surveying her reflection in the long bathroom mirror adjoining one of the guest suites.

God, she thought incredulously. How had she got herself into this mess? She'd had no intention of staying at the Novak house any longer than was necessary. Yet here she was, committed to having dinner with Matt and his family. Committed to spending an evening fighting off Adrienne's hostility and Matt's magnetic appeal.

But only an evening. When Matt had suggested she should stay at the villa, she'd reminded him that she'd booked a room at the Corcovado already. Otherwise God knew what Matt might have expected of her. To share his suite of rooms, perhaps? She couldn't deny an involuntary shiver at the thought.

It was all Adrienne's fault, she decided. The way Matt's mother had reacted when she'd seen her daughter-in-law had put Joanna's nerves on edge. The woman had obviously never expected her to come to Miami. And why not? Matt was usually based in New York.

The situation hadn't improved when Matt had accused her of interfering. 'I believe you knew Joanna was trying to get in touch with me,' he'd said harshly, getting to his feet. 'When were you planning on telling me about that?'

And, when she had evidently been lost for an answer, he'd continued, 'Oh, and what happened to the messages I asked you to send to Joanna? Can I assume they didn't make it either?'

'Don't be sarcastic, Matthew!' Adrienne's face had become even redder than when she'd first seen her daughter-in-law. 'I didn't want you tearing off to London when you'd been so ill. I can assure you, anything I've done has been with your best interests at heart.'

Well, at least that explained why she'd said nothing, Joanna conceded. And perhaps, in the circumstances, she'd had a point.

'So you have been screening my mail.' Matt hadn't been inclined to be tolerant, and the look Adrienne had bestowed on Joanna then showed a little of the anger she was trying so hard to suppress.

'As I've just said, I didn't think you were well enough to deal with your—*wife's*—problems.' There had been a distinct hesitation before the word 'wife'. 'I would have told you, Matt. Eventually. I never suspected she'd turn up here, uninvited.'

Joanna had gasped at this, getting to her feet to

confront the other woman. 'I didn't want to come here,' she'd said tersely. 'Your daughter invited me. She was kind enough to tell me that Matt had been ill.'

'As if you care.'

Adrienne had spoken contemptuously, only to be taken aback when Matt had intervened. 'That's enough,' he'd said grimly. 'Joanna's here now. And whether you attempted to thwart her efforts to get in touch with me or not, I think she deserves some respect, don't you?'

Joanna doubted Adrienne thought any such thing, but she'd known when to give up. The fact that Matt had defended her must have been a bitter pill for her to swallow, and just for a moment Joanna had been tempted to wrap her arms around his neck and pretend she'd come here to forgive him after all.

But that would have been foolish. Not to mention giving Matt entirely the wrong idea. Until she'd told him why she was here, she had to keep her distance. If only Adrienne didn't arouse such a reckless desire for revenge.

Matt's invitation to stay for dinner had been unavoidable.

'But I need to change,' she'd protested. 'My things are still in the suitcase in Sophie's car. Why don't I call a taxi for now, check in at the hotel, and come back again tomorrow? It will give you a chance to read my emails, and then we can discuss why I'm here.'

'What a good idea,' Adrienne had inserted eagerly, but Matt would have none of it.

'I'm not asking you to move in,' he'd said shortly. 'Surely you can pull a change of clothes out of your case. Then you can have a shower and rest for a while until the meal is ready. I do know how exhausting jet lag can be.'

So here she was, Joanna reflected, preparing to join the rest of the family for the evening meal. But her reflection in the mirror filled her with regret. She hadn't brought any formal clothes with her and the simple sage-green silk tunic, which she'd planned on teaming with a pair of black leggings to travel home the next day, ended several revealing inches above her knees. Without the leggings—which were too hot to wear tonight—she'd never been more conscious of her bare legs.

There was no doubt that Adrienne wouldn't like it; might even think Joanna had chosen something purposely provocative to wear. Which was so far from the truth, it was laughable. The last thing Joanna wanted was to have Matt think she'd had second thoughts about the divorce.

And yet, when he'd reached for her hand...

But she refused to entertain such treacherous thoughts. She was sure the problems in their relationship would have developed whether her father had been involved or not.

The rift between them had probably begun to crystallise when her father's company was found to be in difficulties. They'd only been married for a couple of years and, unbeknown to Joanna, Carlyle Construction had been struggling with financial problems for equally as long. It was before Angus Carlyle had been diagnosed with cancer that he'd welcomed NovCo's assistance. It had been the only way to avoid insolvency and debt.

However, after the takeover, her father had insisted his difficulties had arisen because of the downturn in the economy, though Matt had told her they'd existed long before that. At the time, Joanna had been so grateful to Matt for his support that she hadn't questioned his assessment. It had been enough to know her father was solvent again, that Carlyle Construction lived on.

Until the disaster in the Alaskan oilfield.

Two men had been killed and several more injured when a drilling platform owned by NovCo had caught fire. It had made all the newspapers on both sides of the Atlantic, with horrifying pictures of the rescue that had taken place. Joanna had been desperate to speak to her husband, to assure herself that he was well and to learn the truth about the incident. But Matt had been working in New York, and had been tied up in meetings with the offshore oil and gas authorities, and had promised they'd talk in more length when he got back.

And then, when she'd visited her father, who had been in hospital at the time, he'd told her—with some reluctance, he'd insisted—that the real reason Matt didn't want to talk was because he was trying to blame Carlyle Construction for the accident. He'd assured her that he'd never have told her what was going on if Matt hadn't betrayed him. As it was, he couldn't let her think the worst of her father when it wasn't his fault.

Unfortunately, it had been another week before Matt had returned from New York. He'd told Joanna when he expected to return, but that was all, and she hadn't wanted to discuss her father's affairs over the phone when she hadn't known who might be listening. Matt had apologised for not being in touch, but he'd said he'd explain everything when he saw her. He'd finished by telling her he loved her, and not to discuss the accident with anyone until he got back.

When he had got back, she hadn't waited before confronting him with what her father had said. She'd been terribly upset, of course, and in hindsight she should have been more willing to listen to Matt's side of the argument. But her father had been dying, and she couldn't bear to let Angus go on thinking that Matt was blaming him for what had happened.

Matt had been taken aback by her accusations. His revelation that her father had been cutting corners for years, that, prior to the takeover, Carlyle Construction had been struggling because her father had been spending money he didn't have, had stunned her. Matt had also claimed that Angus was simply trying to pre-empt the inevitable investigation into the accident that he knew would prove him guilty. But Angus had been unaware that, in an effort to save her father's reputation, Matt had already briefed the board that NovCo would be accepting all liability for the fire.

However, when she'd told her father what Matt had said, Angus Carlyle had burst into tears. She'd thought at first it was gratitude, but, with his eyes streaming, he'd claimed that, far from protecting him, Matt was deceiving her, too. Angus had friends in New York, he'd said, friends who'd already told him that his name was toxic in the oil-producing community. The authorities were already investigating Carlyle Construction's involvement and it was only a matter of time before NovCo shifted the blame.

His final plea had been that she was his daughter. Whatever differences they'd had in the past, their love for one another had never faltered. And Joanna had known she couldn't deny the words of a man who was suffering with terminal cancer. Particularly as she'd always suspected how determined to protect the company's interests Matt could be.

There'd been a huge row with Matt telling her she had no idea what her father was capable of, and Joanna accusing him of using Angus as a way to save NovCo's reputation. Then she'd stormed out of their apartment, declaring she never wanted to speak to him again.

Learning, weeks later, that NovCo had, in fact, settled all claims against the company had been little compensation. As far as her father had been concerned, Matt had been trying to save his marriage, and had realised he'd made a terrible mistake by accusing him. Angus had even challenged her to ask Matt to explain why he'd hacked into her father's emails, if it wasn't to create a record of phony deals with risky suppliers he was supposed to have made.

She'd phoned Matt but he'd denied it, of course, although he hadn't been able to deny that he had had Angus's financial dealings investigated. But when Joanna had asked him why, he'd refused to answer her. He'd told her to ask her father that question; to put the old man on the spot.

However, Angus had had a relapse, and Joanna hadn't been able to talk to him. And by the time he was in a temporary remission, Matt had been called back to New York.

The weeks of their separation had turned into months. Her father's death had left her devastated, and she couldn't help blaming Matt for ruining the last weeks of his life. David Bellamy had been a hero, helping to organise the funeral for her and offering her her old job back. A situation she'd been glad to accept when she'd discovered her father had been practically destitute when he died.

Turning from the mirror, she went into the bedroom and tried to distract herself by admiring the beauty of her surroundings. Pale walls, pale rugs, and a pale satin bedspread on the wide colonial bed. The colour in the bedroom was provided by exotically patterned cushions and curtains. Paintings of Indian masks and other spiritual objects on the walls were meant to remind the visitor of the area's Native American heritage.

The house was two-storey, stuccoed, with a red-tiled roof and grounds spread over a couple of acres at the end of a gated cul-de-sac. The whole area was criss-crossed by canals, where just occasionally you might glimpse a manatee. The drive leading up to Matt's parents' house ended beside a mission-style Spanish fountain. The steady splash of water on the mossy layers of stone was always present, creating a soothing retreat from the busy world outside.

Joanna had been here before, visiting his parents on a couple of occasions. Though remembering Adrienne's attitude towards her then, she hadn't been sorry to avoid them in recent months.

All the same, the suite Adrienne had reluctantly provided for her use was very appealing. It was all very civilised; very inviting. Nevertheless, Joanna knew that without Adrienne's intrusion she'd have told Matt immediately what she wanted and hightailed it back to the hotel. That had been the plan, anyway. The only thing was, after learning how he still felt about her, she doubted he'd have been willing to grant her request.

She had to come up with a Plan B. Tomorrow afternoon, she'd intended to fly back to London.

The trouble was, by giving in to his request to stay for dinner, she didn't have time to devise an alternative plan.

A faint draught of warm air drifted in through the open windows. Ivory sheers shifted sensuously, and Joanna moved the curtains aside to slide back the long French doors.

Stepping out onto her own private balcony, she breathed in the exotic scents from the garden. Lilies, fuchsias, the heady scent of night jasmine. The humidity was great, as it always was at this time of the year. Early summer in England was not the most appealing time to come to Florida.

Perhaps she should just cut her losses and leave.

The arrival of a maid to tell her drinks were being served in the family room downstairs baulked that possibility. This was it, she thought. Fight or flight? Well, she'd never been a coward, and surely nothing Adrienne Novak said could hurt her now.

As she walked along the landing to the curving marble staircase she saw no one. Below, the marble-tiled foyer was deserted, too. The family room was to her right, a comfortable space, with leather chairs and sofas. A drinks cabinet offered refreshment, and an elegant baby grand piano stood beside the windows at the other side of the room.

When Joanna paused in the doorway, she could smell the flowers that filled the tiled hearth, and the not unpleasant aromas of alcohol and tobacco. But the room itself appeared to be unoccupied as well.

Like the foyer, the lighting was mellow and subdued, and it wasn't surprising that Joanna thought she was alone. But then a figure emerged from the shadows beside the fireplace. A tall figure, lean and saturnine, in a suit and shirt so dark a grey they appeared black.

Matt.

CHAPTER THREE

JOANNA'S MOUTH DRIED. Surely, they were not dining alone.

'Jo,' Matt said, moving towards her, his low voice so familiar, so disturbing to her ears that she caught her breath. 'You look refreshed. Did you rest for a while?'

'Just for a few minutes,' said Joanna, well aware that she hadn't relaxed at all. His clean masculine scent drifted to her nostrils but she endeavoured to ignore it. 'Where is—' she almost said 'your mother', before amending it to '—everyone?'

'They're coming,' said Matt smoothly. He surveyed her with dark expressive eyes. 'You look very beautiful this evening, Jo.'

'Thank you.' But Joanna stiffened, touching the low neckline of the tunic with a nervous finger. She was tempted to check the hemline, too, to pull it further down if that was possible, but she restrained herself. 'Um—how long has Sophie been here?' she asked, desperate to keep their conversation from becoming personal. 'Is she staying long?'

'As long as my mother is prepared to have her,' he replied drily. 'Since the divorce, she spends a lot of time here.'

Joanna nodded. Sophie and her ex-husband had divorced before Matt's father had been taken ill. Joanna had wondered if the break-up of Sophie's marriage had contributed to Oliver Novak's stroke.

'Well—it was nice to see her again,' Joanna continued, when the silence became unbearable. She paused, and then, refusing to be diverted, 'Did your mother show you my emails at last?'

Matt's eyes darkened. 'I assume that's your way of asking if I now know why you're here.'

Joanna shrugged. 'I would have preferred to speak to you in private. That was why I planned to stay at the hotel.'

'There's no hurry.' Matt lifted his shoulders indifferently. 'Let me get you a drink. That might help you to relax.'

'I am relaxed.' Though of course she wasn't. Joanna's lips tightened. 'Why can't we get right to the point?'

Matt ignored her outburst, approaching the drinks cabinet and holding up a bottle of Chardonnay for her inspection. With some misgivings, she nodded, and as he poured he added smoothly, 'You are still my wife, Jo. That gives me some privileges, I think.'

He handed her a glass and she took it with great care, avoiding touching his fingers. Then, after swallowing a mouthful of wine, she tried again. 'You know I didn't want to come here.'

Matt sighed. 'Believe it or not, but I'd gathered that. Don't you think we should take a little time to talk about this?'

'What is there to talk about?' asked Joanna tightly. 'I want a divorce. It's as simple as that.'

'What a pity.' Matt spoke neutrally. 'And here was I, hoping you might stay for a couple of days.'

Joanna stared at him. 'You are joking!'

'No.' Matt was annoyingly composed.

Joanna's lips tightened. 'You can't possibly expect me to stay here when—when your mother obviously hates my guts!'

Matt shrugged. 'And is that the only reason you're declining my invitation?'

'Of course not.' Joanna was frustrated. 'I just don't think there's any point in dragging this out.'

Matt was silent for a moment, and then he added tersely, 'You know, I could do without your animosity. These past few weeks, recovering from that blasted bug, have been hell on earth, believe me.'

'I'm sure they have, Matt, but—'

'But you're not interested.' Matt's tone had roughened with emotion, and, closing the short distance between them, his hands gripped the tops of her bare arms and he drew her towards him. 'This isn't over, Jo,' he said. 'Not nearly.' And before she could do more than draw a startled breath, he bent his head and kissed her mouth.

'Matt!'

The word was muffled and her glass was in serious danger of spilling its contents over the Indian rug. She endeavoured to take a step back, but he was too strong for her. His tongue brushed her lips, and when she resisted his efforts to enter her mouth, he growled his frustration.

'I still want you,' he said, staring down at her, and, God help her, Joanna felt her knees go weak.

'Don't,' she said, hearing the huskiness in her voice, but unable to do anything about it. 'This is not why I made this trip.'

'I know.' Matt released her abruptly and turned away, and she staggered a little as she tried to save her wine. 'I just don't believe our marriage is over.'

Joanna caught her breath. She was annoyingly

aware that she'd bitten her tongue in her efforts to calm herself. 'We've lived apart for almost a year, Matt.'

'What does that prove?' Matt snorted. 'We've been living on different continents, sure, but the connection between us never relied on distance, did it?'

'Matt, please. This is getting us nowhere.'

Forced to look away, she touched the tip of her tongue with an exploring finger, feeling for the blood she was sure she could taste. She was totally unaware of how provocative her action was until she saw Matt watching her, following her probing finger with his eyes.

Oh, Lord!

Pulling her hand away from her mouth, she noticed, belatedly, that he didn't have a glass. And, in an effort to change the subject, she said shortly, 'Aren't you joining me?'

'Alcohol and drugs don't mix,' he replied flatly. 'Now, do you want to tell me why you want a divorce?'

Taking another swallow of wine, she added tensely, 'Let's not do this, Matt.'

Matt's lips twisted. 'I'm sure you're aware that divorces in this country are ten a penny.' He paused. 'Provided they are uncontested.'

'I do know that, yes.'

'So, you expect me to roll over, right? Isn't that what you said in your emails?' His eyes swept insolently over her, and she was supremely conscious of the flimsy fabric of the tunic and her bare legs beneath. 'I have to say, you don't waste words.'

Joanna sighed, guessing Adrienne had shown him one of the later messages she'd sent when impatience had made her less tactful than before. 'I don't believe I said I expected you to roll over,' she responded defensively. 'I thought you were deliberately ignoring me.'

'As you would.' Matt was sardonic. 'But you're my wife, Joanna, and if I have my way, you will remain so.'

'You can't make me,' she said, and then could have bitten her tongue—metaphorically this time—at the childishness of her words.

She attempted to take another gulp of her wine and was dismayed to find the glass was empty. She took a steadying breath. She was allowing him to get the upper hand, and she'd only had one glass.

Matt hesitated, and just when she was afraid he was going to touch her again, he lifted his hands in a defeated gesture and crossed the room to seat himself at the piano.

With his fingers running idly over the keys, he said, 'Tell me, why didn't you touch any of the funds I deposited to your bank account in London?' He paused. 'You didn't have to go back to work at Bellamy's gallery.'

'I wanted to.' Joanna found herself approaching the drinks cabinet and lifting the bottle of Chardonnay. 'I don't need your money, Matt,' she assured him, filling her glass. 'I told you that when—when—'

'When you stormed out of our apartment in London?' Matt suggested mildly, the strains of an old George Michael song emerging from the keys. 'I know what you said, Jo. Your words are imprinted on my soul.'

Joanna shivered in spite of the warmth of the evening. 'Do you have a soul, Matt?' she queried, trying to be flippant, and then gasped in dismay when he slammed the lid of the piano and got to his feet.

'You'd better believe it,' he snapped, covering the space between them so quickly that Joanna, who had been drifting unknowingly towards the music, suddenly found him only inches away. 'I am not the devil incarnate, Jo, no matter what lies your father told you.'

'Don't bring Daddy into this.'

'Why not? He's the real villain here, as far as I'm concerned.'

'He's dead,' said Joanna defensively. 'You can't blame a dead man for your mistakes.'

'My mistakes?' Matt was angry. 'You are such a cliché, do you know that? You keep bringing up trivial things that have no bearing on this conversation. In an effort to try and justify what Angus did.'

'He didn't do anything wrong!'

'Oh, I know that's what you think. I heard the eulogies at his funeral.' Matt was bitter. 'I was there at the funeral, Jo. You didn't know that, did you? I was tactful enough to guess you wouldn't want to see me. But I saw you, Joanna, with Bellamy.'

'David's a good friend,' Joanna protested, but Matt ignored her words.

Joanna had always denied that the gallery owner had any feelings for her, but it was Bellamy she'd turned to when Angus Carlyle had died; Bellamy who'd re-employed her and probably found her somewhere else to live.

She'd moved out of their London apartment,

probably afraid he might turn up and demand his rights as her husband. As if he'd ever done anything but protect her interests.

Anger gave way to frustration, and, to Joanna's alarm, his hand came to cup her face. His thumb brushed the high colour nesting on her cheekbones and then found the startled contours of her mouth.

He'd barely touched her, but Joanna felt as if he were branding her. Almost without her volition, her lips parted, and she tasted him on her tongue. The heat spreading from his fingers seared her throat and breasts, breasts that were suddenly swollen and taut with need.

There was a tingling sensation in the pit of her stomach, too, as nervous tension gripped her abdomen. She felt her muscles tighten, her breath grow shallow, as an unwilling awareness of her vulnerability where this man was concerned weakened her knees.

She was gripping her glass with slippery fingers, and realised she was losing control.

Matt was staring at her, and awareness flared like a flame between them, burning them with its fire. She didn't honestly know what might have happened next if someone hadn't interrupted them; if another voice hadn't chosen that moment to coldly break the spell.

'For God's sake, Matt! What is going on?'

Adrienne's voice was shrill and accusatory, and Joanna despised herself for allowing such a situation to develop. Whatever defence she'd had before would be as nothing now. His mother was bound to think she'd had an ulterior motive for coming here.

Matt, however, seemed indifferent to his mother's arrival. Although he drew back from Joanna, his response revealed his impatience at her words. 'Keep out of it, Ma,' he said, his hand lingering in the small of Joanna's back. 'This has nothing to do with you.'

Adrienne looked wounded. 'Matt!' she protested, and, although her son still looked grim, he got control of himself.

Apparently intending to placate her, he released Joanna and said curtly, 'Do you want a drink?'

His mother was evidently in two minds, but she chose the least provoking option. 'Wine, please,' she said, her gaze flickering over Joanna's glass. 'I'll have red, if you don't mind.'

Joanna was drinking white, but she was so relieved that Matt had moved away from her that she didn't make any comment. In any case, it was just another attempt to annoy her, and she wouldn't give Adrienne the satisfaction of retaliation.

Taking the time to study her adversary, she had to admit the woman had changed little in the year since they'd last met. Adrienne's dark hair might owe more to her hairdresser these days than it did to nature. But her slender build gave her a youthful appearance. If only her hostility towards her daughter-in-law didn't draw her mouth into that thin hostile line.

Matt handed his mother her glass and refilled Joanna's without her permission. But, what the hell? she thought recklessly, taking another gulp of the deliciously cool liquid. She needed all the courage, real or artificial, that she could get.

After drinking a little of her wine, Adrienne turned to Joanna again. 'Sophie tells me you're staying at the Corcovado. How long are you planning to stay in Miami?'

Joanna shrugged. 'Until tomorrow.' She refused to prevaricate, even if she sensed Matt's anger at her words.

Adrienne forced a tight smile. 'Perhaps you should have let us know you were coming.'

'Why?' Joanna was tired of defending herself.

'So you could have kept that news from Matt, as well?'

Adrienne gasped. 'How dare you?' she began, but Matt broke in before she could continue.

'It's the truth, Ma, and you know it. I'll let you know how long Jo is staying after we've talked.'

He returned the bottle of white wine to its tray, his eyes boring into Joanna's, cautioning her not to argue with him. And, although she would have liked to refute his words, there was still a certain pleasure to be had in thwarting his mother.

Adrienne's lips thinned. 'I understood from your correspondence that you intended to ask Matt for a divorce. I don't see what there is to talk about.'

Joanna would have answered her, but Matt chose to intervene. 'If you hadn't chosen to keep Joanna's correspondence to yourself, I might have phoned her,' he said mildly. His hand returned to the sensitive hollow of Joanna's spine. 'As it is, we have the opportunity to speak to one another face to face.'

Once again, Joanna attempted to move away from him to dislodge those cool fingers that were threatening to unnerve her. But her breathless silence was an admission of his dominance, nevertheless. And although it galled her to admit it, she knew that right now he had the upper hand.

'I'm sure Dad would be most disappointed if we didn't make her welcome,' Matt continued, his tone mellowing. Probably because he thought he was getting his own way, thought Joanna, in frustration. 'He was delighted to hear that she was here.'

'You've spoken with your father?' Adrienne was obviously disconcerted and Joanna guessed Matt's mother had hoped to keep her husband in ignorance of what she'd done.

'Of course, I've spoken with him,' responded Matt, as his sister came into the room to join them. He looked again at Joanna. 'Let me refresh your glass.'

Once again, to her dismay, Joanna saw her glass was almost empty. She hadn't been aware of swallowing the wine, but her nerves were all over the place so she obviously had.

'Um—thanks,' she said, ignoring Adrienne's disapproval, and found a smile for her sister-in-law when Sophie complimented her on her dress.

Thankfully, Sophie's arrival did take a little of the pressure off. The young woman might be Matt's sister, but she'd never been able to twist her mother round her little finger as her brother could do. In consequence, Adrienne turned her wrath on her daughter, berating her for not being here sooner and criticising her outfit.

Sophie was wearing a wraparound sheath dress in a rather striking orange linen. Not the shade Joanna would have chosen, but it suited Sophie's dark colouring.

Joanna accepted more wine, but, despite Sophie's friendly chatter, she was overwhelmingly aware of Matt's brooding expression, his dour countenance colouring her mood.

She should have refused his invitation, she thought. Being civil was getting them nowhere. And whatever she did, Adrienne would never compromise.

They ate in a small dining room overlooking the floodlit patio. It was near the kitchen and was much less intimidating than the formal one Joanna remembered when she and Matt were last here. Conversation wasn't easy. The only consolation was that Adrienne disliked the situation as much as she did.

However, when Sophie's attempt to ask her about her work at the art gallery brought a scowl of disapproval from both her mother and her brother, Joanna chose to speak her mind.

Ignoring Matt's warning gaze, she said, 'I enjoy my work, Sophie. I may not be a painter myself, but I have learned to recognise talent when I see it. We—that is the gallery owner and myself— occasionally give unknown painters a showcase for their work. Sort of an amateur exhibition. But you'd be amazed how many of them go on to become professional artists.'

Sophie nodded. 'I envy you, you know. Before I married Jon, I had a job working in the oil business. Not for Dad or Matt, of course. An independent company. And I really enjoyed it. I think I might look for something similar again.'

'Good for you.' Joanna smiled at her. 'I know I'd miss working at the gallery.'

'Well, there are lots of art galleries in New York,' exclaimed Sophie at once. 'Now that you have no ties holding you to London, you could work for one of the galleries there. Don't you agree, Matt?'

Matt didn't answer. Nevertheless, his silence was annoyingly compliant, and Adrienne had heard enough. 'I think not,' she said, giving her daughter an impatient look. 'Joanna isn't staying in Miami, Sophie. She's here to speak to Matt about a—a—' She hesitated uncertainly, obviously aware of Matt's narrow-eyed disapproval. 'Um—about a personal matter,' she finished awkwardly. 'She'll be going back to London tomorrow. Isn't that right, Joanna?'

Before Joanna had a chance to answer, Sophie's face clouded with disappointment. She'd clearly understood what her mother was trying to say. Her jaw dropped as she turned to her brother. 'That's why Joanna booked a room at the Corcovado, isn't it?' she demanded fiercely. 'Don't tell me you've asked her for a divorce?'

CHAPTER FOUR

'I HAVE NOT asked Joanna for a divorce,' Matt responded harshly. 'Not that it's any business of yours, Sophie. Joanna's reasons for being here are not your concern.'

Joanna looked sympathetically at the other girl. 'It's me who wants the divorce,' Joanna said now, ignoring the others. 'It's hardly a secret,' she added, giving Matt a defiant look. 'But thanks for the support.'

'Nevertheless, it is not something to be gossiped about within the hearing of servants,' retorted Adrienne coldly, but now that Sophie had broken the ice, Joanna could stay silent no longer.

'I suggest it's not up to you to decide,' she declared curtly, addressing her mother-in-law. 'Or has reading my husband's emails persuaded you that you should have the final word?'

'If I had you would not be here!' retorted Adrienne at once, but when she looked to her son again, maybe in the hope of his endorsement, it seemed Matt had had enough.

Ignoring all of them, he got up from the table to pour himself another soda, and Joanna couldn't decide whether he was being deliberately rude or simply indifferent.

'Well, I won't intrude on your family any longer,' she declared stiffly, addressing herself to Adrienne as Matt didn't return to the table. 'If you'll excuse me, I need to use the bathroom.'

She'd barely eaten a thing, but she felt sick anyway. A green salad, rich with herbs and sprinkled with parmesan, had been followed by a seafood ravioli that should have melted in her mouth. But all Joanna had been able to think about was how soon this agony would be over. She'd already decided to hand any further negotiations over to the London solicitors, and go back to London on the first available plane.

She left the room without another word, aware that both women were expecting Matt to stop her. But he didn't, although she was sure his eyes followed her progress. With a feeling of relief, she hurried across the foyer and ran up the stairs.

By the time she reached the suite, Joanna's legs were shaky. Her mobile phone was in her bag and she intended to call a taxi to take her back to the hotel immediately. Matt could deal with the fall-out, if there was any. He was very good at that.

Someone had been in the room in her absence. The bed had been turned down, and she wondered who had thought she might be staying the night. Matt, perhaps, she decided tightly. He was very good at ignoring her feelings, too.

After glancing a little tensely around the room, she headed for the bathroom. Despite refusing the dessert, she still felt decidedly unwell. Too many glasses of wine, she thought, peering at her face in the mirror. She only hoped she could get back to the hotel without throwing up.

She was leaning on the hand basin, with her eyes closed, when someone spoke.

'Are you all right?'

Her eyes shot open in alarm. Matt was leaning against the open door of the bathroom, a look of mild concern on his lean dark face. A face she'd once loved, she thought, hating herself for the memory. Had that face betrayed her and her father without a second thought?

Matt had shed his jacket and tie and now the cuffs of his shirt were turned back over lean brown forearms lightly spread with dark hair. Despite her anger at him, she felt her stomach quiver at the unwelcome acknowledgement of his magnetism. Whatever she did, however she felt, she couldn't deny her unwilling response to his sexual appeal.

But this wouldn't do. Schooling her features, she said, 'What are you doing here? I don't recall inviting you in.'

Matt shrugged his broad shoulders, muscles moving sinuously beneath the fine silk of his dark shirt. 'You didn't,' he agreed, and then was forced to step aside as she brushed past him to get into the bedroom. 'Still better in health than temper, I see.'

Joanna pursed her lips. 'Don't make fun of me.'

'Believe it or not, I was concerned about you.' Matt tucked his hands beneath his arms to quell the urge he had to reach out to her. He surveyed her closely. 'Are you sure you're all right? You looked very pale when you left the dining room.'

'I didn't think you'd noticed.'

'I noticed.'

Joanna knew a feeling of defeat. She was never going to win where Matt was concerned. All the same, if she'd suspected he might follow her, she'd have wedged the back of a chair under the handle of the door rather than face another argument.

'Why don't you leave me alone?' she asked

wearily, refusing to give in to the tears that were threatening to complete her humiliation. 'I've ordered a taxi.'

Matt blew out a breath. 'You haven't had time,' he stated flatly. He paused. 'You insist on going back to the hotel, then?'

'Of course. I'm not welcome here.'

'I want you to stay.'

'Yes, I know what you want. But this is your mother's house and I don't intend to stay here any longer than it takes for a taxi to come and pick me up.'

'It's my father's house, but we won't quibble about ownership.' He paused. 'Please. Cancel the room at the hotel and stay. We need to talk.'

'We have talked, Matt.'

'Not enough.' His brows drew together. 'Are you afraid of me, Jo?'

Joanna's lips parted. 'No,' she said defiantly, although she was. Afraid of her own vulnerability where he was concerned at least.

'Yet you insist on running out on me. Again.'

Joanna caught her breath. 'All right,' she said, knowing she'd regret the words as soon as they were spoken. 'We'll talk tomorrow. Come to the hotel in the morning, and we'll have breakfast together. Okay?'

* * *

Half an hour later, Joanna stared out of the window of the sleek Mercedes saloon Matt was driving, amazed at how quiet the streets were at this hour of the evening. But she could hear music thumping from a boom box somewhere and the unmistakeable sound of laughter that seemed to be coming from the roofs of the hotels and apartment buildings they passed.

Not that she was truly interested in the parties being held in high rises and condominiums alike, or the brilliantly illuminated stretches of open parkland on Biscayne Boulevard. It was simply better than acknowledging that once again Matt had got his way.

She should have known he wouldn't let her get away that easily, and she hadn't argued when Matt had told her he would be driving her back to her hotel. Besides, in all honesty, she was glad to be with someone she knew; even her husband. Just in case she did want to throw up.

He'd been waiting for her when she'd come downstairs. Sophie had been with him, and for once her sister-in-law had had little to say. 'I hope we see you soon,' she'd murmured as they'd stepped out into the humid evening air. 'Don't blame Matt for my mother's behaviour, will you?

She's always been ridiculously possessive of her only son.'

As if Joanna didn't know that.

It didn't take long to reach Miami Beach. Matt drove over one of the causeways that separated the Beach from Miami proper and then cruised along Collins Avenue to where the Corcovado Hotel occupied a prime spot overlooking the ocean.

The grounds were spectacular. Acres of palm-strewn patios, outdoor cafés and bars, even an Olympic-size swimming pool, floodlit and busy with holidaymakers.

The humidity seemed more intense when Joanna stepped out of the car. Matt had brought the Mercedes to a halt under the awning by the entrance to the hotel, and Joanna didn't waste any time before hurrying towards the automatic doors.

Her casual 'See you tomorrow' should have sealed the deal. But the doors had hardly closed behind her before she became aware that someone else was on her heels.

Glancing round, she wasn't surprised to find it was Matt, but that didn't stop her from feeling a surge of resentment at his persistence. 'What do you want now?' she demanded, feeling the heat rising up her face at the knowledge that their conversation could be clearly overheard by other guests. 'I've said I'll see you in the morning and I will.'

Matt's dark brows arched impatiently. 'Did you think I wouldn't escort you to your room?'

'I don't need an escort,' she said, aware that two women, waiting at the check-in desk, were keeping a surreptitious eye on both of them. But most particularly on Matt.

And why not? she thought irritably. Without his jacket, his shirt half unbuttoned because of the heat, he looked far more at home in these luxurious surroundings than she did. Tall and lean, with a touch of the *café-au-lait* skin tone of some distant ancestor, he was perfectly in control of himself and of the situation, she thought.

Joanna tried to avoid looking at him, but it was difficult. Her eyes were irresistibly drawn to the open neckline of his shirt, to the triangle of dark hair visible on his chest. His lips had parted enquiringly, and Joanna felt her instinctive response. They were thin lips, hard and masculine, and Joanna knew they could be both tenderly soft and brutally cruel.

She swallowed. He wasn't moving and she really didn't need this. 'Okay,' she said, fumbling in her bag for the booking information she'd downloaded to her phone. 'You can see me to the lift. But that's all.'

It was only as she studied the phone that she remembered she had still to check in. Learning that Matt had been seriously ill and giving in to Sophie's invitation to drive to the villa, she hadn't confirmed the booking or paid the deposit required, which she'd promised to do as soon as she left the airport. Such trivial details had gone completely out of her head.

What if they'd given her room to someone else? Damn!

Taking a breath, she turned to him and said, 'I've not checked in yet.' She hesitated. 'There's a queue, and there's really no need for you to stay.'

Matt felt the kind of tension he hadn't felt since they were last together. The muscles in his stomach clenched as he said, 'You're sure you have a room here?'

'As sure as I can be.' Joanna didn't want to face the alternative. 'I phoned the hotel from the airport.'

Matt's dark eyes narrowed. 'From the airport?' he echoed incredulously.

Joanna straightened her spine. 'Look, when I left New York, I didn't know if you were staying in Miami. All I knew was that I wouldn't have time to hire a car and drive out to Coral Gables and back in a couple of hours. I was going to phone you, but I needed somewhere to stay, and I remembered—well, I remembered we'd stayed here before.'

'So we did.' Matt's eyes darkened. 'I'm flattered you recall our visits.'

'Don't be sarcastic.' Joanna sighed. 'I suppose I had thoughts of asking you to join me here for dinner.'

'To talk, I assume,' he remarked, still somewhat sarcastically, and Joanna's lips tightened.

'I thought that was what you wanted.'

Matt lifted his shoulders dismissively. 'And Sophie changed your mind?'

'Well, yes.' Joanna took another steadying breath. 'She told me you'd been ill and—and I was concerned.'

'How sweet!'

Matt gave a mocking laugh and rocked back on the heels of his suede loafers. That was the last thing he'd expected her to say.

Joanna resented his reaction. 'I'd be concerned about anyone in similar circumstances,' she declared, avoiding the lazy beauty of his eyes. 'Just because I felt sorry for you—'

Matt grimaced then. 'I don't need anyone to

feel sorry for me,' he told her shortly. 'I've had a surfeit of that already.'

Clicking her tongue impatiently, she stepped up to the end of the line. 'Why don't you just go, Matt?' she demanded, glancing about her. 'You're just wasting your time here.'

'I wouldn't say that,' he countered, and Joanna gave him an exasperated look.

'All right, then,' she said tightly, turning her back on him. 'But you're going to have to wait. I haven't even registered yet.'

'So you said.'

Matt sounded thoughtful, but after a few moments she heard the unmistakeable sound of him walking away. Oh, well, she thought, telling herself she was relieved. It was what she'd wanted. She wouldn't have liked him leaning over her shoulder while she filled in the forms.

When someone touched her arm a few moments later, she swung round, firmly believing Matt had decided to return. But instead it was someone called George Szudek. The Hotel Manager, or so it said on the badge he was wearing on his lapel.

He was a stocky individual, with a bald head and a full beard and moustache. He greeted her with a smile and gently urged her across the lobby to the open door of his office.

'Mrs Novak,' he said politely, guiding her into the room. 'I believe I can be of some assistance to you and your husband.'

CHAPTER FIVE

JOANNA REALISED SHE should have anticipated something like this when Matt disappeared. Because, of course, her husband had been waiting for them in the manager's office.

Matt had been standing by the windows, looking out on the manicured golf course at this side of the hotel. His hands were thrust into the pockets of his pants, his shoulders broad beneath the heat-dampened silk of his shirt.

And despite herself, Joanna felt a pang, not unlike the pang she'd felt when Matt and his father had first walked into the Bellamy Gallery all those years ago.

David had been hosting another of those evenings for new artists, and apparently one of his flyers had found its way into the lobby of the Novaks' hotel. Matt had told her his father had persuaded him to come; light relief after a day of boardroom politics. But he'd told Joanna that as soon as he'd seen her he'd been very glad he had...

* * *

Joanna looked round the gallery with a feeling of pride. The place was full, patrons and visitors milling about, helping themselves to a glass of wine or a canapé, offering silent and not so silent opinions of the paintings on display.

And she'd arranged it all, she thought with pride. She'd sent out the invitations, arranged for flyers to be placed in hotel lobbies, made the event sound so attractive that any visitor to the capital might be intrigued by its originality.

The young artist they were showcasing, Damon Ford, was a minor celebrity in his own right after winning a gold medal in athletics at the last Olympics.

But in spite of this success, Joanna believed that his art was the real attraction here. His work was an abstract palette with no perspective in visual reality. It wasn't to everyone's taste, but in a world where fantasy had become so popular, Damon's imagery struck a chord.

'A good turn-out.'

David Bellamy, the man who owned the gallery and her boss, spoke the words with some satisfaction.

'You've done good, Joanna. Damon should be pleased.'

Joanna smiled. 'Oh, he is. I spoke to him a few moments ago, and he's really excited to see his work enjoying such success. It depends whether anyone buys anything, of course, but I saw the Arts Editor from the Evening Gazette *just now and he seemed very impressed.'*

She looked eagerly about her. Yes, she thought, her instincts had been right. Damon was that unusual thing: an artist who cared, not just about his work, but also about pleasing his public.

Her eyes scanned the crowd as they had been doing all evening and came to rest on two men who had just come in. They were both tall and dark, but the younger man was slightly taller than his companion, with the kind of dark penetrating gaze that sought Joanna out and found her—staring at him.

Oh, God, she thought, looking away, embarrassment filling her face with what she was sure was unbecoming colour. An unfamiliar fluttering began in the pit of her stomach, and she pressed a nervous hand to her midriff. He would think she was trying to attract his attention, when nothing could be further from the truth.

Nevertheless, she managed to appear composed when the man in question pushed his way through the crowd to join her.

'Hi,' he said, with the kind of lazy smile that brought goose bumps out all over her skin, 'I understand you're the artist here.'

His accent revealed he was from the other side of the Atlantic and Joanna was taken aback. 'Oh—oh, no,' she said hurriedly. 'No, I'm not the artist. I just helped to organise the event.'

'That's what I meant,' he said easily. 'This is some classy affair you've put on.'

'Do you think so?' Joanna couldn't help being flattered. It was one thing for David to say she'd done a good job and quite another for one of their guests to compliment her.

'Sure.' He glanced about him. 'So—do you want to show me where can I get a drink around here?'

Nevertheless, she'd quickly realised that it was not the time to be thinking about the past. Matt had heard their entrance and swung round to look at them, and, although she'd been tempted to turn on her heel and march back out of the door, defiance, and the knowledge that she'd only embarrass the manager, had kept her where she was.

In consequence, the man was now opening the door of an invitingly lamplit suite on the eighteenth floor, ushering them both inside, just as if Matt was staying the night.

'If there is anything else I can do for you, Mr Novak,' he said, irritating Joanna anew by addressing Matt, 'you have only to let me know.' He handed him the key card. 'I'm sure you'll be very comfortable here.'

'I'm sure we will,' agreed Matt, his hand compelling Joanna forward, a silent warning not to argue. 'Thanks for your help, George. I won't forget it.'

The manager lifted a self-deprecating hand, and, with another smile in Joanna's direction, he stepped out of the room and closed the door firmly behind him. And the minute the door was closed, Joanna moved abruptly out of Matt's possessive reach.

'I suppose you expect me to be grateful,' she said, aware of the disagreeableness of her tone. 'Well, okay, I appreciate not having to stand in a queue, but I would just as soon be in one of the standard rooms.'

Matt snorted. 'How did I know you were going to say something like that?' He strolled across the sitting room to where sliding glass doors opened onto a private balcony. 'You might like to step outside and admire the view,' he added, glancing back over his shoulder. 'You can hear the ocean from here.'

'And feel the humidity,' retorted Joanna, making no attempt to join him. The manager had carried her bag upstairs and now she picked it up to carry into the adjoining bedroom. But the realisation that Matt would probably follow her if she did had her setting it down again. 'Please, close the windows and go.'

"Aren't you going to offer me a drink? I'd have thought it was the least you could do after the efforts I've made on your behalf,' remarked Matt tolerantly, but he did at least part of what she'd asked and slid the window closed.

Efforts I didn't ask you to make, thought Joanna uncharitably.

Glancing round, she saw the small fridge, masquerading as a polished cabinet.

'Help yourself. You're paying for it.'

Matt crossed the room and plucked a can of cola from inside the cabinet and inclined his head. 'Thanks.'

'My pleasure,' she said, her tone indicating the opposite. Then, she added, 'You're not going to change my mind, you know.'

'Okay.' Matt shrugged. 'But as you said, we'll talk about it in the morning.'

'Is there any point?'

'I hope so.' Matt raised the can to his lips and took a drink, and then looked around the room. 'This reminds me of the suite we occupied the first time I brought you here.' He took the step that allowed him to glance through the bedroom door. 'Yeah, I remember they had to come and change the bed because we'd made love in the shower and we were still soaked when we—'

Joanna's lips tightened. 'Stop it,' she said, unable to deny the images his words had created. She took a steadying breath. 'Is—is your father enjoying his return to work?'

'My father?' If Matt was disconcerted by her segue into another subject entirely, he didn't comment upon it. 'I think he was fairly keen to take over when I was incapacitated, if that's what you mean. My mother less so.'

Joanna draped a hand over the back of a chair. 'So what's new?' she murmured drily. 'Adrienne likes her men to be where she can keep an eye on them.'

'Which would account, I suppose, for her keeping your emails secret. She'd have known I'd have flown to England in a heartbeat if I'd known you wanted to see me.'

Joanna, whose eyes had been glued to the muscles moving in his throat, dragged her gaze away. 'I assume that goes for the messages you supposedly sent me?'

Matt rolled the cool can sensuously against his throat. 'There's no "supposedly" about it,' he declared, and Joanna's eyes were drawn to him again. 'I was beginning to think that you might not want to come and see the invalid.'

'If I'd known...' Joanna began and then broke off.

What if she had known Matt was ill, she wondered, what would she have done? Truthfully, she didn't know.

But Matt wasn't inclined to let her get away with it. 'If you'd known—what? Dare I hope you might have been concerned enough to make the trip for that reason and that reason alone?'

Joanna had to be honest. 'I really don't know.'

'You'd have been too busy?'

'No. But I wouldn't have thought you'd want to see me.'

'I see.' Matt considered her response, and then offered a segue of his own. 'Tell me, is Bellamy still playing a prominent role in your life?'

Joanna swallowed. 'Please, leave David out of this.'

Matt's eyes glittered. 'So tell me, how do you fill your time? Going to the theatre? Visiting the gym?'

'I have friends,' said Joanna curtly. 'And occasionally we eat out together. Not David,' she added, seeing his expression. 'Other friends. And I've spent some time with Mum and Lionel.'

'Have you?' Matt was impressed. 'I thought you didn't get on.'

Joanna hesitated. 'Things are different now.'

'Since your father died?' Matt enquired sardonically. 'Yes, I can believe that. You know, I always felt sorry for your mother. Angus had virtually cut her off from her only offspring. And all because he was jealous.'

'Don't say that.'

'Why? It's the truth. He never forgave Glenys for leaving him and he used you to get his revenge.'

'No!'

Matt shrugged. 'Have it your way,' he said wearily. 'One day you'll come to your senses and see the truth. That explosion off the Alaskan coast wasn't the fault of NovCo. We didn't become as successful as we have by cutting corners on our equipment.'

'Nor did Daddy,' she countered hotly and for a moment Matt was inclined to let it go.

But, dear God, she'd believed Angus's lies for over a year, and Matt was damned if he was going to let her go on believing her father was an angel.

'So did Angus tell you we paid the hefty penalty the Alaskan authorities demanded out of the goodness of our hearts?' He shook his head. 'It was to protect you, Joanna. I know you don't believe me, but your father had been cheating his workforce for years.'

Joanna felt a shiver of apprehension slide down her spine. What if she was wrong? What if her father had been lying? She wrapped her arms about herself, needing the protection. 'I don't want to talk about this, Matt.'

'No, I bet you bloody don't.' Matt was angry now and he didn't think before grasping one of her arms and jerking her round to face him. 'You can't accept the truth when it's staring you in the face.' His hot breath fanned across her cheek. 'Damn you, Joanna. I swore I wouldn't do this, but I care about you.'

Joanna lips parted. She hadn't expected him to say that. Her heart was racing and she could feel the perspiration trickling down her spine. 'I'm only here because I want a divorce,' she insisted doggedly. 'Not to rehash old grievances.'

'You're afraid to face the truth,' retorted Matt

harshly. 'You're letting your father ruin your life.'
His lean fingers dug into the bones of her shoulders. 'Wherever he is right now, I bet the old devil is clapping his hands at your naivety.'

'Daddy said you only married me to get control of his company.'

Matt's eyes narrowed. 'You and I were an item long before Angus decided to use me to get him out of the hole he'd dug for himself.'

Joanna and Matt married only six months after they'd met at the gallery showing. Matt knew her father didn't approve of the speed with which they'd got together—nor did his mother, if it came to that—but he and Joanna were in love and nothing else seemed to matter.

And those first few months they were deliriously happy.

They honeymooned in Fiji and then moved into the apartment Matt had acquired on the Upper East Side of New York. They had an apartment in London, too, but it was the New York apartment that they regarded as home.

And it was a beautiful apartment, overlooking the East river, with plenty of room for themselves and a family when it came along. They had staff in both places, but Joanna liked looking after her husband herself. And the dinner parties she gave accrued many compliments from friends and business colleagues alike.

Matt suspected the fact that Joanna didn't get pregnant during the second year of their marriage was a significant contribution to the problems that came after. He knew she wanted a baby, and he wanted it too, but two things happened in swift succession to make it even harder for them to have their wish.

To begin with Oliver Novak had a stroke, which meant Matt had to spend more and more time controlling NovCo. And then Joanna's father's company was found to be in financial difficulties, necessitating a buy-out that Matt organised on Joanna's behalf.

Matt knew Angus Carlyle resented having to ask his son-in-law for help, but Matt thought it was worth it to see the relief in Joanna's face. Even so, he found it hard to keep the real circumstances of Carlyle Construction's problems from her. Particularly as he guessed Angus would find some way to pay him back.

Having a baby still eluded them, however, and making love became a mechanical thing, subject to times of the month and temperatures, and not the joyful declaration of their love for one an-

other that it used to be. They argued more when they were together, and Matt knew his wife was retreating more and more into her shell.

Her father being diagnosed with lung cancer was devastating. It meant Joanna moved into the London apartment on a permanent basis, unwilling to leave her father on his own when he had no one else. Matt didn't like to think it, but he sensed she was relieved to move out of the New York apartment. In London, she didn't have to face any of the albeit well-meaning questions about her possible pregnancy that she'd had to face from their friends in New York.

The disaster in the Alaskan oilfield came only weeks after Angus's cancer diagnosis. Matt hadn't thought at that time that it would prove the straw that broke the camel's back. But then he'd had no idea that Angus would use the accident to destroy their marriage. He would never have believed a man in his position could be so completely cruel.

Who was it who said that no good deed ever went unpunished? Matt thought now, putting his memories of the past aside. He'd been a fool, and he knew it. But, God help him, he wanted Joanna to see the truth.

CHAPTER SIX

'WHY DON'T YOU just accept the situation and move on?' Joanna was saying now, and Matt gave a weary shake of his head.

'Move on to what?' He was annoyingly persistent.

'I don't know. Another woman, perhaps.' Although that thought still had the power to upset her. 'The—the one who's been keeping your bed warm since we split up. You can't pretend you've been lonely since I walked out.'

Matt's eyes darkened. 'How would you know that?'

'I read the tabloids, Matt. I've seen the pictures of you with other women. You're not exactly back-page news.'

Matt arched a mocking brow. 'Jealous?'

'Of course not.' Although she had been, if she was totally honest. 'Naturally I was interested,' she added, trying to sound offhand. 'You have your own life to lead. I—I never expected you to live the life of a monk.'

Matt shook his head. He had the feeling she was never going to admit to the chemistry that still flared between them. Ignoring her resistance, he cupped her nape with his free hand, tipping her face up to his.

'Tell me you don't want me to kiss you,' he grated roughly. 'Tell me you don't want to feel the thrust of my body taking possession of yours, and I'll let you go.'

Joanna sucked in a breath; he was much closer now and twice as provocative. 'You're crazy!'

'Am I?' Matt rotated his hips against hers and she felt the unmistakeable hardness of his arousal. He took the wrist he was holding and wound it behind her back, pressing her even closer. 'You used to like me to do this. You used to like it when I laid you out on the bed and licked my way down—'

'Don't say any more!'

Joanna could hardly get the words out. Against her will, her legs were trembling, and she was unable to prevent the muscled power of his thigh from forcing its way between hers.

It was weakness, pure and simple, she assured

herself, but she was very much afraid he might feel the dampness at her crotch and know she was lying now.

She'd known the attraction she'd always had for him hadn't gone away. That was why she'd fought against coming to the United States in the first place. But God help her, she'd never actually thought she might find herself in a position where she wanted to give in to it again.

Matt's eyes darkened, and instead of lowering his mouth to hers, his expression took on a mocking slant. 'You know,' he said consideringly, 'I think you would love me to seduce you, if only to prove how desperate I am.' He paused. 'I am right, aren't I?'

Joanna didn't answer, but he could feel the softening of her body, could smell the arousal of her sex. Yet, in spite of the anticipation of her soft flesh yielding to his invasion, Matt managed to push her away.

Forcing the sexual images from his mind, he said harshly, 'You'd love me to make a fool of myself, wouldn't you? To get down on my knees and beg you to change your mind?'

'No!'

The word was practically wrung from her lips, but he didn't believe her.

For a moment, he felt some sympathy, but only for a moment. 'Well, I still have some pride.' His lips twisted. 'I'm out of here, Joanna. If you still want to talk in the morning, I'll meet you for breakfast. Your choice. Goodnight.'

Joanna caught her lower lip between her teeth as he strode towards the door.

'I didn't want to talk to begin with,' she shouted after him, needing to defend herself. 'You've got a whole different scenario going on here and you're making me take the blame for your mistakes.'

His smile was mocking. 'Yeah, you go on believing that. Personally, I don't give a damn.'

Joanna pursed her lips. 'I don't know why you're saying these things,' she persisted. 'I didn't ask you to get this suite. I didn't ask you to come up here.'

'No.' He conceded the point. 'I was stupid enough to think you might thank me for making life easier for you. But, I should have known better.'

'Matt!'

He'd reached the door when she called his name, and although he glanced back over his shoulder, his lean dark face was hard and unforgiving.

'Matt.' She couldn't believe she was going to say the words, but she couldn't let him leave without some words of justification. 'Don't go. Not like this.'

Matt's brows ascended. 'Are you saying I was right?'

'No—' Joanna licked dry lips. 'I mean, you can't honestly believe that I want you to seduce me? I simply thought...' She shrugged. 'Can't we still be friends?'

'Friends!' Matt gave a disbelieving laugh as he turned and pressed his back against the door. 'You're not serious?'

Joanna had the feeling that she'd had too many glasses of wine. She wasn't thinking clearly. She'd wanted him to go, for heaven's sake. So why was she delaying him now?

When she didn't answer, Matt got impatient. 'I don't have time for this,' he said roughly. 'I suggest you go to bed. I'll meet you in the coffee bar in the morning.'

Joanna licked her lips. 'What if I don't want to go to bed?' There was so much adrenalin coursing through her veins, she doubted she'd ever sleep again. Instead, she walked towards the windows Matt had opened earlier. 'The pool's floodlit, isn't it? I might go for a swim.'

Matt stared at her as if she'd taken leave of her senses.

But Joanna was suddenly so warm her skin was prickling with heat. Hardly thinking what she was about to do, she unbuttoned her tunic and peeled it off. Then she tipped the straps of her bra down over her arms, feeling the blessed relief of air from the air-conditioning system cooling her over-heated flesh.

Matt swore. 'What the hell do you think you're doing?' he demanded, and she heard the revealing thickening of his tone. His voice was both harsh and raw with emotion, and Joanna lifted a nervous hand to her throat.

'I'm going for a swim,' she said lightly. 'The water will be beautifully cool at this time of the evening.'

Matt's teeth ground together. 'If you think I might come with you—'

'I don't expect anything of you, Matt.' Yet despite her words desire was suddenly shimmering throughout her body. Her blood was racing like liquid fire, and she moistened dry lips with a pink tongue. 'You can stay or go. It's up to you.'

'I made my decision five minutes ago,' Matt reminded her, stifling a curse, but his face suddenly blazed with colour. Didn't she realise what seeing her in only half a bra and a skimpy pair of panties was doing to him?

Of course, she did. He scowled. 'If this is some sick game you're playing—'

'It's no game.' She took a deep breath, stretching her arms above her head. 'I don't play games, Matt. I'm going swimming. What's wrong with that?'

'It's after eleven o'clock.'

'So?'

Matt swore and turned towards the door again and she realised he was really leaving this time. Which was probably just as well, she assured herself unsteadily, grabbing her overnight bag and heading for the bathroom. That way he need never know she'd only been bluffing.

She didn't wait to hear the door slam behind him. There was a closed door to her left, which she guessed led into the bathroom, and she couldn't wait to take off the rest of her clothes and step into a cool shower. She had no illusions now that Matt really cared what happened to her, and she found her eyes were stupidly brimming with tears.

She was reaching for the handle when a lean brown wrist came over her shoulder. Matt's hand flattened against the door, successfully preventing her from opening it.

'You planning on getting changed in the closet?'

he asked, his taut body imprisoning hers against the door. 'Not a good plan, Jo.'

Joanna gulped. 'I thought you were leaving.'

'I was. I should be.' Matt's voice was hoarse. 'But I'm crazy. Didn't you know?'

Aware that her heart was palpitating in her breast, Joanna rested her hot face against the panels of the door. 'Why are you still here?' she whispered brokenly. 'What do you want from me?'

'Don't you know?' Matt demanded savagely. His hand slid beneath her bra, his palm rubbing sensuously over her burgeoning nipple. 'Go on, tell me to go now. Or are you having too much fun at my expense?'

'I'm not having fun at your expense,' protested Joanna, her breath hitching as he lowered his free hand to her stomach. 'I didn't want you to go.'

'You know what, I find that hard to believe.'

'It's true,' she panted, leaning her head back against his shoulder. 'You're still the only man I've ever loved.'

Matt's breath caught in his throat and he allowed his fingers to slide down over the flimsy lace of her panties. Joanna's stomach contracted, and she shuddered in anticipation when his hand continued down until it was trapped between her legs.

Then he pressed her back against his throbbing

shaft and muttered in an undertone, 'Now I guess you know why I'm still here,' as he swung her round to face him. Then he bent his head and took possession of her mouth.

And Joanna knew that ever since she'd seen Matt again, she'd been fighting this battle over and over in her mind. Now she didn't hesitate, giving herself up to the demands of her senses, winding her arms around his neck and parting her lips for his tongue.

Her lacy bra was discarded, and his tongue tugging on her nipples was a forbidden delight. Tiny rivulets of fire invaded every pore of her body, and she dragged his mouth back to hers with an urgency too long denied.

Her fingers sought the button at the waist of his pants and she caressed his taut stomach with her knuckles as she pulled it free. Then his zip slid smoothly down to his crotch and exposed the bulging outline of his shaft.

His erection swelled against the silk of his boxers. She half expected him to take her there, pressed against the door. She wouldn't have objected, she thought wildly. But he inhaled a tortuous breath and swung her up into his arms.

'The bed, I think,' he said thickly, and, stepping over his pants, he carried her into the room next door.

Between lowering her onto the bed and following her down he managed to dispose of his boxers. Then, straddling her yielding form, he cupped her face between his hands. 'If you change your mind now, I'll never forgive you,' he muttered hoarsely, but Joanna's fingers were already seeking the swollen stiffness of his shaft.

'I need to be inside you. God, why did you make me wait so long?' he choked, almost strangled by his emotions.

Just for a brief moment, as Matt's tongue traced a sensuous path from her breasts to her navel and beyond, Joanna wondered if it was she who was crazy and not him. How would she feel about this in the morning? Would she remember it as the biggest mistake of her life? But when his fingers slipped between her legs again and entered her, she arched to meet them. Then shuddered as a wave of sexual pleasure sent her hurtling over the brink.

She wrapped her arms and legs around him, and he didn't hesitate. With an urgency born of need, he moved between her thighs and buried his length inside her.

Their lovemaking was hot and passionate. Matt

had forgotten how good it felt to be with her, to have her muscles tightening around him, her body tensing again, ready for what was to come. When he felt the spasms of excitement rippling through her, he pushed ever more deeply into her core.

Joanna's head was spinning. She'd missed Matt's lovemaking more than she could ever say. Their rhythms matched, so smooth, so natural. Her body arched to meet his thrusts, perfectly in tune with his demands.

When he moved faster, so did she. She felt as if her senses were on overload, spiralling out of control. The darkness of his passion surrounded her, the pulse of his excitement causing her to climax again and again. And when his release came, she clung to him, feeling him filling her with his seed.

Joanna opened her eyes to daylight.

It was still very early. Barely six o'clock according to her watch. But attuned as she was to British time, the fact that the sun was not yet up meant nothing. Miami was five hours behind London and in consequence she was instantly wide awake.

She blinked as her brain kicked in, recognising the suite at the hotel the manager had shown them into the night before. She and Matt, she remembered, with a sudden feeling of apprehension.

Dear God!

Propping herself up on her elbows, she turned her head, half expecting to find herself alone. Surely what she'd thought had happened had been just a dream; a sensual hallucination; brought about by overwrought senses and too many glasses of wine.

But she was not alone. There was a warm body beside hers in the bed. Matt's body, she realised a little incredulously, as her breathing quickened in disbelief. He'd evidently fallen asleep, as she had. So what price now her earlier conviction that she'd imagined the whole thing?

Easing back against the pillows, not wanting to disturb him until she'd assessed the situation, she felt a headache probing at her temples. Evidently, she'd had too many glasses of wine and too little sustenance the night before. Why else, in the name of all that was holy, would she have allowed this to happen? After everything she'd said about her husband, how had she got herself into this mess?

The awareness of her own nakedness briefly diverted her. She hadn't slept in the nude since the last time she and Matt had shared a bed. She certainly hadn't expected to share one with him again. Not on this trip. Nor any other. What about her demands for a divorce?

The ache between her thighs was a reminder of what had actually occurred. They'd made love several times, she remembered, her skin prickling in response. They'd both seemed insatiable, she recalled, unable to deny it. She'd wanted him, quite desperately as it had turned out. So what did that say about her?

She might hate Matt for the way she believed he'd betrayed her father, but he'd now know it hadn't entirely erased the feelings they'd once shared. If only she'd taken David's advice and conducted this negotiation from a distance. Yet she couldn't entirely blame Matt for her own weakness where he was concerned.

She lifted a hand to her breasts. They, too, were intensely sensitive, and she recalled how Matt had suckled from their swollen peaks. Then his mouth had burned a sensual path to her navel, before he'd buried his head so erotically between her thighs.

Involuntarily, her hand slid down to touch the damp curls between her legs. She was sensitive there, too. But it was just sex, she told herself fiercely. Sex that had driven her to behave the way she had. Nothing more.

Yet seeing Matt's head on the pillow beside hers,

she knew she couldn't trust herself to behave any more sensibly this morning. Wanting someone was an addictive thing, and she was apparently unable to resist. She was intensely vulnerable, so she should make sure she wasn't here when he woke up.

For a moment more, she studied his lean dark features, fighting the lingering desire to draw his hand between her legs. She couldn't deny he was still immensely attractive to her, but she believed the love she'd once had for him had given way to a much more basic need.

It wouldn't last, she assured herself. No relationship built on such foundations survived. The sooner she collected her belongings and got out of the hotel, the better.

What a blessing it was that she hadn't unpacked the night before, she thought, as she slid cautiously out of bed. Although she'd left her jeans and tee shirt on the bed when she'd gone to dinner at the villa, she'd stuffed them back into her bag before leaving for the hotel.

A quick use of the facilities and she could be on her way, she thought. Though it was nerve-racking trying to get dressed without disturbing Matt. She had no idea what she'd say to him if he woke up. Or what he might say to her.

But he didn't wake up. He was still sleeping soundly when she headed for the door. She hesitated for a moment in the doorway, wishing it didn't have to end like this. Then, squaring her shoulders, she slipped the latch and headed for the lift.

CHAPTER SEVEN

JOANNA WAS EXHAUSTED by the time she let herself into her small apartment the following morning. The flight from New York had landed soon after six-thirty. And, although she'd been hoping to get a few hours' sleep on the flight, a crying baby and the man beside her snoring for most of the journey had put paid to that.

She'd flown home via New York because the flight from Miami to London hadn't been due to leave until the evening and the last thing she'd wanted to do was hang around Miami airport, looking as though she was waiting for Matt to come and find her.

There'd been a flight to New York almost immediately, and she'd been lucky enough to snag a seat in business class. She'd excused the extravagance on the grounds that it was an emergency. Some things were worth the price you had to pay.

She wasn't looking forward to seeing David again. Naturally she wouldn't tell him she'd slept with Matt. But she was very much afraid he would suspect what had been going on. And in her present fragile state, she might well reveal more than she intended.

He was bound to say 'I told you so' if she admitted that the visit hadn't gone as she'd anticipated. He'd warned her not to go and she half wished she'd taken his advice.

Half wished?

Shaking her head, she stripped off her clothes and headed for the shower. Standing under the hot spray, she felt as if she was sluicing every trace of Matt's lovemaking from her body. A vain hope, she acknowledged, and when she heard the phone ringing as she turned off the water, she found herself hoping that it was Matt.

Crazily, her heart skipped a beat at the thought, but then she quickly came down to earth again. It was her mobile phone that was ringing and Matt didn't have her mobile number. Wrapping a bath towel around her, she went with rather less enthusiasm to answer it, which even she knew was foolish. She felt a sense of resignation when she saw David Bellamy's number on the small screen.

She really didn't want to talk to him right now. Yet she had no choice. 'Hi, David,' she said, trying to adopt an upbeat tone. Crossing her fingers to protect herself against the lie, she added, 'I was going to ring you later.'

'How much later?' He didn't sound appeased. 'You must have arrived home hours ago.'

'Not hours,' she protested. 'It was early morning when I landed. You might not have been awake if I'd phoned you then.'

'Even so...'

'David, I needed a shower and a change of clothes. You know what it's like when you've been away.'

'You were only away a couple of days, Joanna. It was hardly a holiday.' He sighed. 'Do I take it you saw the great man?'

'I saw Matt, yes.' Joanna hesitated before continuing. 'Actually, he's been ill. That's why he didn't answer any of my emails.'

'Really?'

'Yes, really,' she said, half annoyed at feeling the need to defend herself. 'He'd picked up a bug in South America while he was there.'

'Oh, well...' David evidently decided not to push his luck. 'So you'll be coming in—what? Later today?'

'Make it tomorrow,' she said, although the idea of going into work at all wasn't appealing right now. 'This place is a mess and I need to do some grocery shopping.' She paused. 'Is that all right?'

'I guess so,' replied David ruefully. 'Anyway, I just wanted to assure myself that you got home safely.'

'Well, thanks.' Joanna realised she'd been in danger of taking her frustrations out on him. 'I'll tell you all about my trip tomorrow.' Or as much as was sensible anyway. 'Okay?'

It was the hotel phone that awakened Matt.

His own mobile phone was in the pocket of the trousers he'd taken off—well, kicked off in the other room, actually—the night before. If it had rung earlier, he certainly hadn't heard it.

Groaning, he blinked, taking stock of his surroundings. Then, realising that Joanna wasn't beside him—was she in the shower? —he rolled over to snag the phone at her side of the bed.

'Yeah?'

'Matt? Oh, thank goodness, I've reached you at last. I've been ringing your phone for ages but you didn't answer.'

Matt recognised his sister's voice at once. 'What's the urgency?'

Sophie clicked her tongue. 'Well, when you

didn't come home last night, we were all concerned. But then, this business with Dad—'

'What business with Dad?' Matt dragged himself up against the pillows and forced himself to
focus on what she was saying. 'What's happened?'

Sophie sighed. 'Oh, Matt, we had a call from
Andy Reichert in the early hours.' Andy Reichert
was his—now his father's—second-in-command.
'He'd phoned Dad last night, and he'd been concerned when he couldn't reach him. Apparently,
Dad hadn't been too well during the afternoon,
so, as a last resort, Andy went to the office.

'He found Dad slumped over his desk. He called
911, naturally, and Dad was rushed to hospital.
It's another stroke, Matt. A more serious one this
time. No one knows what the eventual outcome
will be, but right now it's touch and go.'

Three weeks later, Joanna had accepted that Matt
wasn't going to contact her. Whatever had happened in Miami, he'd evidently decided there was
no point in pursuing her to England.

She'd found it hard to accept at first. She'd been
so sure he'd want to see her again. Foolish, perhaps, but after the night they'd spent together,
she'd actually been tempted to give him a second chance.

Still, maybe that was just her hormones talking. Whatever, she'd finally convinced herself that maintaining the status quo was in her best interests and his. She'd been in danger of losing sight of her reasons for going to Miami in the first place. Was she so easy to deceive?

Evidently so.

She hadn't heard from Matt's solicitors either, though in the last week, and with David's encouragement, she'd consulted a firm of divorce lawyers here in London. She'd given them Matt's address and had assumed they'd contact him on her behalf, and she'd waited on tenterhooks for his response. But nothing had come of it. Yet.

A second interview was planned for the beginning of the following week, and she'd decide then what she was going to do. There didn't seem much point in delaying the inevitable. Which meant she had to tell her mother what was going on.

Glenys Carlyle—or Glenys Avery, as she was now—lived in Cornwall with her second husband. Lionel Avery was a wine merchant she'd met at a night club in London fifteen years ago, just after she and Joanna's father had separated.

Although he was almost eight years her junior, they seemed happy together. And despite the fact that Joanna had initially resented her mother for leaving her father, time, and the fallout both before and after her father's death, had strengthened their relationship.

She'd been fourteen when her parents split up, and whenever the topic had come up, her father had always blamed his ex-wife. It was true, her mother had been the one to walk out on the marriage, but it was also true that Angus Carlyle was not the easiest man to live with.

After Glenys and Lionel were married, her mother had invited Joanna to live with them. But Joanna had felt she couldn't leave her father on his own. Okay, she'd acknowledged that Angus Carlyle had his faults, but she didn't feel she could abandon him completely.

And she hadn't. But she found herself wondering now if that had been her first mistake.

Matt landed in London at about seven p.m. He'd used the company jet to fly to England, rather than try to book a seat on the scheduled flight, but he hadn't been able to relax. Too much was going on, both in his business and his personal life. His pilot hadn't been too pleased at being hauled out of bed in the early hours of the morning either, but he'd known better than to cause a fuss.

Matt had received the divorce papers from Joanna's solicitors a few days ago, and since then he'd been agitating to get away. But he had responsibilities. Since his father's second stroke, he'd had to take over again as CEO of the company, and it had been impossible for him to drop everything to fly to London.

A company car was waiting for him at the airport, and he gave the driver Joanna's current address. Although he still owned the apartment they had shared in the city, she didn't live there. After their break-up, she'd found her own apartment not far from the gallery. With Bellamy's help, no doubt, Matt thought dourly, as the limousine transported him swiftly through the busy streets.

Colgate Court was a small development of one- and two-bedroomed serviced apartments, with the amenities common to such accommodations. Matt scowled when he got out of the car, reflecting that if Joanna had been willing to use the money he'd deposited regularly in her bank account, she could have afforded somewhere a lot better than this.

But it was adequate, he conceded, bending to inform his driver that he'd ring him if he needed him again. Then, fastening a couple of buttons on his cashmere jacket, he strode quickly towards the entry.

Matt had never been inside the building before, but he had checked the place out after attending her father's funeral. He'd wanted to know where she was living, particularly as Joanna had apparently changed the number of her mobile phone so he couldn't reach her that way.

A man was standing in the lobby of the building, looking out at him. The door to one of the ground-floor apartments was ajar and Matt wondered if he was the caretaker for the building. The outer door was locked with the usual keypad beside it, and after ascertaining which apartment was occupied by Mrs—no, *Ms*—Carlyle, he scowled at the anomaly and pressed her bell.

There was no response and his scowl deepened. He'd been fairly sure she'd be at home at this hour of the evening. Perhaps the man would know. He hesitated only a moment before knocking at the door, and after a second's hesitation the man came to open it.

However, he regarded Matt rather suspiciously, as if he wasn't used to dealing with visitors after dark. Especially a tall, intimidating visitor, who was regarding him with a definite air of impatience.

Matt's skin was darkly tanned, too, after his convalescence in Florida, and he had an unconscious arrogance that apparently aroused the man's defences. 'Can I help you?' he asked offhandedly, and Matt got the feeling that he was hoping he'd say no.

'You already have,' Matt replied, thrusting his hands into the pockets of his jacket. Then, without waiting for an invitation, he stepped inside, causing the man to back up in alarm.

Adopting his most unthreatening tone, Matt continued, 'I'm here to visit with my wife, Mrs Novak? Um, that is—Ms Carlyle,' he amended shortly. 'Do you know if she's at home?'

The man frowned, and tucked the newspaper he'd been carrying under his arm. 'I wouldn't know,' he said, with evident satisfaction. 'I'm only the caretaker here. Sorry.'

Matt knew an almost uncontrollable desire to swear, but instead he said stiffly, 'I'll go up and see for myself. The third floor, isn't it?'

The man took a heavy breath. 'I can't let you do that. You can ring her bell again, if you like, but—'

Matt controlled his annoyance with an effort. 'She might have been in the bathroom when I rang,' he protested.

'She might indeed.' The man sniffed and Matt sucked in an impatient breath.

'Mrs—*Ms* Carlyle is my wife,' he said curtly. 'I need to speak with her.'

'Do you now?' The man cleared his throat. 'Does she know you're coming?'

Matt's hands curled into fists in his pockets. He wasn't used to being treated in this way. 'No,' he snapped tersely. 'Not that it's any business of yours. Now, if you'll—'

But before he could go on, the door to a lift he'd barely noticed before swept open at the other side of the lobby. Footsteps crossed the faux marble floor, halting uncertainly when he turned.

'Matt!'

Joanna was standing just a few yards from the lift. She was carrying what appeared to be a basket of laundry, and he guessed she'd been on her way to speak to the caretaker. Why else bring a basket of laundry down to the ground floor?

But now she'd halted and was staring at him with disbelieving eyes.

She was so beautiful, he thought. Her streaked blonde curls shone like gold, as if the sun were hidden in their heavy masses. Her eyes were wide and startled as she gazed at him, twin orbs of a deep blue, surrounded by long darkened lashes.

'Hello, Joanna,' he said, resisting the urge to glance triumphantly at his companion. 'Perhaps you would tell our nervous friend here that we're acquainted?'

CHAPTER EIGHT

JOANNA MOISTENED LIPS that had suddenly become as dry as the desert. 'Um—yes, Mr Johnson,' she said, with evident reluctance, Matt thought. 'I know Mr Novak.'

'Novak?' The older man frowned. 'He said his name was Carlyle.'

'No, you've assumed that,' Matt contradicted him shortly, getting tired of this fruitless exchange. 'However, she is my wife.' He arched his dark brows at Joanna. 'Am I right?'

Joanna hesitated, but, aware that the caretaker was watching their exchange, she said, 'For the present.'

She heaved a breath, and then spoke again to the man. 'Actually, I wanted to tell you I'm going away tomorrow for a few days.' She might wish she hadn't chosen this particular moment to give the caretaker this news, but it was too late now. She'd been on her way back from the laundry in the basement and it had seemed the ideal opportunity. 'Would you mind keeping an eye on the apartment for me, Mr Johnson?'

'No problem, Ms Carlyle,' he said, annoying Matt anew with his familiarity. 'I hope you're going somewhere warm. It's been so cold these last few days.'

'Hasn't it?'

Joanna managed a smile before heading back towards the lift, with Matt following her. But although he evidently expected her to press the button, she stopped and turned to face him instead. 'Well?'

'Well?' he said blankly. 'Well, what?'

'I assume you came here to talk to me. So, go ahead, talk.'

'Not here.' Matt's patience was shredding. 'I suggest we go up to your apartment.'

Joanna squared her shoulders and glanced at her watch—the slim Patek Philippe watch, he'd given her, Matt noticed, reassured that she hadn't abandoned it along with everything else. 'I'm sorry,' she said stiffly, 'that's not convenient. You should have given me some warning that you were coming to England.'

'As you warned me you were coming to Miami?' suggested Matt tensely. 'What's wrong?

Do you already have a visitor? Is my arrival inconvenient?'

Joanna pursed her lips. 'No—and yes,' she replied, shifting a little nervously. 'What do you want, Matt? It's a bit late for a social call.'

'Is it?'

Matt was sardonic, and Joanna gave a weary sigh. 'It is when I have things to do.'

'Because you're going away?'

'Yes. You've just heard that I'm going away tomorrow.' He noticed she was avoiding his gaze. 'I still need to tidy the apartment and finish my packing.'

Matt scowled. 'Where are you going?' His eyes narrowed. 'More to the point, who are you going with?'

Joanna smoothed the laundry in the basket. 'Does it matter? We decided some time ago that our relationship is over.'

'Did we? Was that before or after you got me into bed?'

'I didn't—' Joanna broke off, wondering what he'd say if she told him she'd been expecting him to contact her for the past three weeks. 'I hope you're not anticipating another one-night stand.'

'I'm not.' His voice was harsh.

But, in truth, his feelings for her hadn't changed.

Yet why would he expect a warm welcome? It had taken him three weeks to come and find her and she didn't know why.

As if sensing his frustration, she finally pressed the button to summon the lift. When the doors opened and she stepped inside, he followed her. She definitely didn't want to cause a scene. Besides, ridiculous as it seemed, she was glad to see Matt.

But unfortunately, that reminded her of how he'd looked the last time she'd seen him, naked in bed. And she definitely shouldn't be thinking about that now. He did look a little weary, however, but he was still a disturbingly handsome man.

In charcoal pants and an olive-green buttoned sweater, a black cashmere jacket accentuating the powerful width of his shoulders, he was achingly familiar. His attractive features were in no way diminished by the hard line of his mouth. A mouth that had always—always—been fascinating to her. She even found herself wondering if the reason he hadn't contacted her was because he'd had a recurrence of his illness.

God, why did she care?

'So, are you going to tell me where you're

going?' he asked, as she pressed the button for the third floor. 'Or is it a state secret?'

Joanna sighed. 'I'm going to Cornwall,' she said, trying to keep focussed. 'I'm going to spend a few days with my mother and Lionel. It's some time since I've seen them.'

'Really?' Matt's tone was even. 'Does Glenys know you want a divorce?'

'We haven't discussed it, no.' Joanna spoke quickly. She'd been avoiding that conversation in fact. Her mother knew they were separated, but Joanna had never debated the reasons with her. Glenys had always been fond of Matt, and Joanna had known she would likely take his side if she told her what Angus had said.

Matt's brows arched enquiringly. 'Why haven't you told her before now?'

Joanna drew in a breath. 'Because, I haven't,' she said shortly, catching herself before she admitted the truth. 'I'm taking the morning train to Truro. I intend to tell her while I'm there.'

The lift stopped at the third floor before Matt could answer. But, just in case she had any notion of scurrying into her apartment and locking him out, he took the basket of clean laundry out of her hands.

'Let me,' he said, with restrained courtesy. 'It's the least I can do.'

Joanna made no response. What would be the point? If he'd taken the trouble to come here, he evidently had something to say.

'I could come with you,' he offered, as she fumbled in the pocket of her tight jeans for her key. 'I'd like to see Glenys again.'

'You're joking!' Joanna cast a startled look over her shoulder. 'Don't you have work to do?'

Matt wasn't deterred. 'Perhaps I'd enjoy a break. I have been to Cornwall before.'

Of course, he had. When Joanna and Matt were first married, both Glenys and Lionel Avery had made them very welcome in both their London home and the house in Padsworth.

These days the Averys lived permanently in the small fishing village not far from Truro. Although Lionel still commuted to London once a month to check on his wine-importing business, he and Glenys had made a very comfortable life for themselves in Cornwall.

With some misgivings, Joanna opened the door into the apartment and Matt followed her inside. He had never been to the apartment before, and she would have preferred to keep it that way. Apart from the fact that it was small and rather shabby, there were no disturbing images to upset her here. No lingering memories of the life they'd once shared.

Now that would change. Now that he'd filled the place with his masculinity and his magnetism, it was never going to feel the same again. The small foyer that gave onto a studio-type space, serving as both kitchen and living room, was dwarfed by his presence. She could only be grateful he'd have no reason to go into her bedroom or its adjoining bath.

For his part, Matt looked about him with interest. Cream walls, a terracotta-coloured carpet, a green sofa with a matching easy chair. It didn't bear any resemblance to the luxurious apartment they'd once shared in Knightsbridge, but it was cosy. And Matt guessed that for Joanna it represented independence.

He looked at her now as she snatched the basket of clothes out of his hands, and stood with it in her arms. Even when she was wearing frayed jeans and a skimpy tee shirt he found her fascinating. But her mood was less so, and she regarded him with wary eyes.

'I don't want you to come to Cornwall with me,' she said stiffly. 'Mum and Lionel would get the wrong idea.'

'And that would be?'

'That I've changed my mind about the divorce,' she declared staunchly.

'But you've just said they don't know anything about it.' Matt's tone was dry. 'So they could hardly get the wrong idea.'

Joanna pursed her lips. 'They'll know soon enough.' She paused. 'And I haven't changed my mind, so there's no point in pretending otherwise.'

Matt regarded her narrowly. 'At the risk of another argument, I'd say you're pretty good at giving people the wrong idea.'

'Because of what happened in Miami?' Joanna could feel her cheeks burning. 'That—that was a one-off. It won't happen again.'

Matt was sardonic. 'Gee, you've no idea how good that makes me feel.'

'It wasn't like that.' Joanna bent her head. 'It just happened.'

'The result of too much wine and adrenalin, is that it?'

'Something like that.' Joanna moved to set the basket of laundry on the kitchen counter. She tried not to be daunted by his height, or the way he towered over her in her trainers. 'I suppose you're wondering why I didn't stick around until you'd woken up?'

'Well, that would be a start.' Matt regarded her with dark enquiring eyes. 'Or were you afraid of what might happen if I did?'

'You flatter yourself,' said Joanna tartly, but she was glad he couldn't read her thoughts. 'As you say, I'd had too much to drink and I was—I was embarrassed about how I'd behaved.'

Matt gave an incredulous laugh. 'Are you in the habit of having sex with men when you've had too much to drink?'

'No.' Joanna was indignant. 'I've never done anything like that before, and you should know it. And I didn't have sex with *men*! You were—*you still are*—my husband. It was foolish, but—life happens.'

Doesn't it just? mused Matt grimly, wondering why he'd ever thought she'd want to see him again. Right now, he had the mother of all headaches, and a belated belief that he'd made yet another mistake.

'So, tell me,' he said, 'why didn't you just let me go? If you're so desperate to get a divorce, it would have been the simplest thing to do.'

Joanna stifled a groan. Didn't she know it? What madness had gripped her? All she knew was that she'd revealed a side of herself she hadn't even known existed. That Matt hadn't known existed. And she wasn't proud of it.

Oh, God!

With a feeling of defeat, she wrapped her arms around herself. If only she'd left for Cornwall this morning before Matt chose to come here and humiliate her again.

Matt brooded now, his brows descending over eyes as dark as midnight. 'I simply don't understand.'

'I know.' Joanna pressed her hands together. And then another thought occurred to her. 'Anyway,' she added, 'you've taken long enough to decide you wanted to see me again.'

'I have, haven't I?' Matt's tone hardened with his words. 'I had my reasons.'

'Maybe there was some other woman you had to get rid of first,' suggested Joanna, achieving an air of indifference she was far from feeling. 'Should I be flattered that you're here at all?'

'Don't try to be clever,' said Matt wearily. 'There is no other woman.' He paused. 'You can't blame me because you lost your nerve.'

Joanna wished she had his skill in always having an answer. His ability to peel the skin from her flesh with his words left her feeling raw and exposed.

'Anyway, I bet you were on the phone to the airport before you even had a shower!' she retorted, seeking vindication. 'You could have found me before now, if that's what you'd really wanted to do.'

'Is that what you expected?'

'No!' Her flush deepened, but she had to be honest. 'Well, perhaps.'

'Really?' Matt suddenly recalled the phone call he'd received from Sophie with a shudder of revulsion. 'Well, perhaps I would have done just that, but, as I said before—something came up.'

Joanna shrugged with what she hoped looked like acceptance. Not looking at him, she pulled some of the clothes out of the basket and started folding towels and underwear. 'So what distracted you?' she asked, unable to leave it alone. 'If it wasn't a woman—'

Matt's eyes were suddenly as cold as ice chips. 'As a matter of fact, I got a call that my father had had another stroke. Forgive me, but that news kind of took precedence over everything else.'

CHAPTER NINE

JOANNA'S JAW DROPPED and she stopped what she was doing to stare at him. 'Oliver—has had another stroke?' she echoed faintly. She had always been fond of Matt's father. 'I—I'm so sorry. I had no idea. How is he? Not—not—'

'Dead?' Matt's voice was bitter now. 'No, he's still living. Barely, at the moment, but that's more his fault than anyone else's.'

Joanna frowned. 'Surely he wants to get better?'

'You'd think so, wouldn't you?'

Matt shook his head, wondering if she deserved an explanation. He wandered over to the windows that overlooked the parking lot, staring out with unseeing eyes.

Then, when the silence in the apartment had become almost palpable, he said flatly, 'The stroke has left him partially paralysed this time. He has little feeling in the left side of his body. He can't dress himself or drive, which means there's no way he can live alone, as he's been doing while I was ill. Consequently, he can't carry on the pretence of running NovCo.'

Joanna's own problems were briefly diverted by his words. 'But why would he want to? I thought you would—'

'What?' Matt turned to face her again, hands pushing his jacket aside to slide into the pockets of his pants, pulling the fabric taut across his groin. 'What did you think, Joanna? That I'd be taking over again, now that I've recovered from the bug?'

Joanna swallowed, her eyes irresistibly drawn to the bulge beneath his zip. Forcing herself to look away, she struggled to stay focussed. 'I—I assumed you would.'

'Well, you were wrong.' He shook his head. 'I'm leaving the company. Sophie's going to take over as CEO.'

'Sophie!' Joanna was staggered.

Matt shrugged. 'She was always more interested in making money than I was, but Dad never took her seriously before. Talking to you seems to have given her the incentive to do what she wants for a change. She only got married to please my mother, but now that she and Jon have split up, and Dad's not in a position to object, she's getting her chance.'

Joanna could hardly believe it. Occasionally,

when they'd still been together, Matt had spoken of leaving NovCo and doing something else. But she'd never believed he would.

'I'll maintain an interest, of course, and so will my father,' he continued. 'It will still mainly be a family concern. But I've realised I want more out of life than spending my days sitting in board-rooms, and my nights socialising with people who are only interested in me because of what they think I can do for them.'

Joanna tried to make sense of what he was say-ing. 'And—and this is why your father isn't re-covering as he should?' she asked, picking up a thong with hands that weren't quite steady.

'Partly.' Matt's eyes flickered over the scrap of lace she was holding, and Joanna thrust it back into the basket in the hope that he hadn't seen what it was. 'I'd warned him weeks ago, when I first got back from Venezuela, that I was consid-ering retiring from the company,' Matt continued, as if that little embarrassment hadn't taken place. 'But he didn't believe a word of it until now.'

'I'm sure.' Joanna was grateful for the chance to distract him. 'Poor Oliver.'

'Well, I can't take all the blame.' Matt's lips twisted. 'The old man wants his independence back and it's not going to happen. But he will improve if he listens to his doctors and the physios who are trying to help him.'

Joanna shook her head. 'He must feel so helpless.'

'Yeah. I guess. But once he realises I'm serious about moving down to the Bahamas, and he sees that Sophie's doing a good job, he'll come around.'

Joanna stared at him disbelievingly. 'What on earth are you going to do in the Bahamas? You'll be bored stiff.'

'Hardly.' Matt was impatient. 'I'm thinking I might write a novel. Goodness knows, I've got plenty of ideas after recent events. But for now, I'm planning on catering to weekend yachtsmen and those who enjoy deep-sea fishing. I intend to buy a couple of franchises. It'll be a change of pace, if nothing else.'

Joanna had to admit, she was shocked. 'So, you're giving up running NovCo altogether,' she said, still trying to get her head round the idea. 'I always thought it was your life.'

'You were my life.' Matt's dark gaze was compelling. 'When you left, I started to realise how narrow my world had become.'

'Are you saying I did you a favour?' she asked incredulously, and Matt gave her a scornful look.

'It was a wake-up call,' he answered. 'I suppose

Angus did me that service at least. Hell, Joanna, I had hoped you'd have come to your senses before now.' Matt expelled a weary breath. 'But I guess I should have known better. You are your father's daughter, after all.'

'What's that supposed to mean?' Joanna spoke defensively, and Matt groaned.

'Joanna, thanks to NovCo, the millions of dollars in compensation resulting from Carlyle's botched construction have been paid. Something your father couldn't have done, even if he'd wanted to. Do you honestly think we'd have bought your old man's company if we'd known he was cheating on his contracts? For God's sake, Joanna, have a bit of sense.'

'It was the rig NovCo installed that caught fire.'

'NovCo installed it, but they didn't build it.' Matt was bitter. 'When the salvage operators got down to the wrecked platform, the spec on the burned outer casing proved it had come from your father's workshop.'

'Daddy said you'd changed the records to protect yourselves.'

'As he would. But how do you change something like a bar code? That's something I'd like to know.'

'Well, if Daddy was still here, maybe he could tell you.'

Matt blew out a weary breath. They'd had this argument before and he knew he was wasting his time. Even if his desire for her was forcing him to try and reason with her again, he knew he'd never convince her that he was right. But he'd get over it, he assured himself. He'd control that as he'd controlled so much else in the past few months.

She was looking anxious now, and he relented. 'Let's forget it,' he said. 'What I choose to do now is no longer your concern.'

Joanna hesitated. 'This novel you're thinking of writing: it has nothing to do with the accident, does it?' Joanna dragged her lower lip between her teeth. 'I mean, I know you hate me—'

Matt expelled a tired breath. 'I don't hate you, Jo. I think your loyalties are misplaced, but I'd never do anything to hurt you.'

Joanna was reassured, but there was still another question she had to ask. 'Why didn't you tell me what you were planning to do when I saw you?'

'When?' Matt replied. 'When you came to the villa and accused me of ignoring your emails? Or that night at the hotel when you hauled me into bed.' He shook his head. 'You had other things on your mind.'

Joanna could feel her face reddening. 'And if I did, you were more than willing.'

'There is that.' Matt's lips twisted. 'I don't deny I was pretty out of it myself. We definitely had something special.' He paused. 'If you remember, we always did.'

Joanna did remember. She felt a constriction in her throat and turned her attention back to the laundry. 'Sex isn't everything,' she murmured, half hoping he wouldn't hear her. But he had.

'You keep telling yourself that.' Matt was tired of trying to get through to her. He dragged a hand through his hair and allowed it to rest at the back of his neck. Then he regarded her with disillusioned eyes. 'You know what? That's it. I'm out of here.'

He shook his head. He should have realised that if she'd wanted to see him again, she'd have stayed in Miami. But after their night together, he'd actually hoped she might have had a change of heart.

He had to wonder how she'd react if he told her that since the takeover of Carlyle Construction, he'd been protecting her father's reputation. He doubted she'd believe that either, but the temptation to explode the saintly myth she'd created about her father was almost irresistible.

Angus was so grateful when Matt rescued the company. He got the old man out of a hole so deep he had to wonder how he'd got there in the first place.

But that didn't trouble him until later. Businesses did fail, he knew that, and he'd never suspected that it was her father's addiction to gambling that was to blame. He doubted he'd have found out at all if it hadn't been for NovCo's accountants. Naturally Angus's financial statements had been audited, and his dirty little secret had been exposed.

Of course, when Matt had found out Angus had begged him not to tell anyone, particularly Joanna. And had it not been for the fact that Matt himself had arranged for it to be concealed the reasons behind Carlyle Construction's collapse would have been disclosed. Even Oliver had been doubtful of his son's magnanimity. Matt had broken the law himself to give his father-in-law a second chance.

In the meantime Angus promised to give up his online gambling. And because there was no way Matt could enrol him in Gamblers Anonymous without everyone finding out what had happened he'd had to trust the old man to keep his word.

Matt had known how much this would upset his wife if she learned of her father's addiction. In consequence, Matt had destroyed all the evidence of the old man's guilt and kept it to himself.

Until he'd discovered for the first time that Angus's word meant nothing at all.

Thinking about it now, Matt abandoned any hope of appealing to her. Let her go on believing he had lied to her. He no longer had the will to care.

'I'll send you my new address, should you need to get in touch with me,' Matt said at last, feeling his headache worsening. He lifted a hand as she started to protest, and added, 'It's a courtesy, nothing more.' He squared his shoulders. 'Have a good life, Joanna. I, for one, intend to do the same. But in spite of everything, I'll never regret those years we spent together.'

He wondered in passing what she thought her father had done with the millions he'd made out of selling his business to NovCo. Without thinking it through, he let his tongue get the better of his good sense.

'This apartment's okay,' he said casually. 'But I'd have expected you to spend some of the money

Angus left you. He owned his own house, didn't he? And he was still getting a dividend from his shares.'

'The solicitor said—' she started. And then broke off before saying shortly, 'Don't concern yourself on my account. I'm quite happy here.'

I doubt it, thought Matt tiredly. But apparently common sense had died along with everything else.

Cursing his conscience, Matt took a step towards her and for a moment Joanna was sure he was going to pull her into his arms. His lean dark face was suddenly too close to hers and she could smell the subtle tang of his deodorant, mingling with the faintly musky odour of his skin.

And right then, all she could think about was how powerful he was and how wonderful it had felt to have his arms around her again. She couldn't help herself, she swayed towards him, but he put out a hand to keep her at bay.

'Not again, Jo,' he said roughly, his fingers curling around her wrist. 'It's too late. I've got no intention of being your fall guy again.'

'You were never my fall guy.' Joanna could feel a sense of panic gripping her at the knowledge that if he walked out of here now, she might never see him again. 'Matt—'

But he wasn't listening. Releasing her, he started for the door. Then obviously against his will, he turned back to cup her neck and drag her towards him. He bent his head and took her mouth almost savagely. It was a hard kiss, almost as cruel as his fingers, but her senses swam as soon as he lifted his head.

'You can have your divorce,' he told her harshly, despising the urge he still had to take her to bed. 'I'll have my lawyers contact yours as soon as I get back to the States. I just hope it keeps you warm on all those cold nights to come.'

CHAPTER TEN

JOANNA WAS CROUCHED over the toilet in the bathroom when she heard someone knock at her bedroom door.

It could only be her mother, she thought unhappily, dragging herself to her feet. Glenys had been worried about her the night before when she'd thrown up after supper. Evidently the fact that Joanna hadn't as yet come down for breakfast had added to her concern.

When she emerged from the bathroom, her mother was standing in the bedroom doorway, her blue eyes, not unlike Joanna's, narrowed in dismay. 'Oh, darling,' she said. 'Have you been sick again? Do you think it was that risotto we had for supper yesterday evening? Lionel swore those prawns were fresh that morning, but, I must admit, I had my doubts.'

Joanna blew out a breath and managed to straighten her shoulders. It was tempting to let her mother go on thinking that it was something she'd eaten that had caused her upset stomach.

But it wasn't. She'd been fighting off the truth for over three weeks now. And it wasn't going to go away.

'I'm sure the risotto was fine,' she said, putting off the moment. 'You look nice,' she added, in an effort to divert herself. And it was true, in a pink silk tee and short dungarees, her mother looked younger than she'd done for years.

'Thank you, darling.'

Glenys smiled her pleasure and, moving to the mirror above the vanity, Joanna gave her own appearance a critical appraisal. The loose-fitting tank and khaki shorts hid the slightly enlarged shape of her breasts, which her mother might or might not notice. Pushing back her hair, she twisted it into a careless knot and then turned to face her mother again.

Glenys looked anxious. 'Are you still planning on going back to London tomorrow?'

Joanna bit her lip. 'I have to,' she said, managing a smile. 'And I have enjoyed this break. It was just what I needed.'

'Well, I must admit I was delighted when you said you were coming down again. Two visits in less than a month. It must be a record.' She paused. 'Is it anything to do with Matt?'

'Why should you think that?'

'Oh, I don't know.' Her mother looked anxious. 'Has he been to see you again?'

'No.' Joanna was defensive. 'I told you, Matt and I are getting a divorce.'

'Well, I know what you said...but ever since you got here a few days ago, I've felt you had something on your mind.'

And of course, she had.

'David is expecting me back,' Joanna said now, trying to change the subject. 'August is a busy month, and he does pay my salary, you know.'

Glenys snorted. 'Surely, you're not going to pretend you need the money, Joanna. Despite what you say about Matt, I'm sure he gives you a generous allowance.

'I don't take money from Matt.'

'Well, I'm sure your father left you comfortably off, then,' exclaimed her mother impatiently. 'I remember you telling me that Matt's company paid him millions of dollars for Carlyle Construction.'

Joanna didn't want to think about that, particularly after what Matt had said.

She couldn't deny she'd been surprised when her father's solicitor had told her Angus had been virtually bankrupt when he died. Even the house he'd lived in, and where Joanna had spent her childhood, was mortgaged to the hilt. There'd been a little cash, which had eventually cleared probate. But she couldn't think where all the money might have gone.

'I like my job,' she said, avoiding her mother's comment. 'I like my independence.'

'Nevertheless, Lionel and I worry about you living in London on your own.'

Joanna sighed, and then decided she couldn't put it off any longer. 'I won't be on my own much longer,' she said, and saw the way her mother's eyes widened in surprise.

With a wry smile, she continued, 'I think I'm pregnant, Mum. I need to go back to London to see my doctor. To prove that the two pregnancy tests I took were not—'

'You're pregnant!' Her mother didn't let her finish. 'Oh, Joanna, am I going to be a grandmother at last?' And then, with rather less enthusiasm, 'I suppose David Bellamy is the father.'

'No!' Joanna was appalled that her mother should think such a thing. 'David's a friend, that's all. Look, I didn't want to tell you this, but he's already got a partner. A male partner. But, please, keep that to yourself.'

'Of course.' But her mother looked only partially relieved. 'Then who?'

'It's Matt's, of course,' said Joanna flatly. 'We spent the night together when I was in Miami. Go figure!'

Glenys stared at her daughter. 'But—I thought you said you went to ask him for a divorce.'

'I did.'

'I can't believe it.' Glenys struggled for words. 'All those years you were trying for a baby...' Her voice trailed away and she shook her head.

'It just happened, that's all. As you say, we'd tried so long to have a baby, I had no idea I'd get pregnant so easily.'

'Still, there must be something between you two if you spent a night together,' Glenys protested. 'Have you told him yet?'

'No. How could I?' Joanna wished her mother weren't so delighted by the news. 'It—it was a mistake, Mum,' she said flatly. 'Now I've got to figure out what I'm going to do.'

'But it's good news, surely,' exclaimed her mother. 'You and Matt have always wanted a family.'

'Yes, but it's not me and Matt any more.' Joanna expelled a shaky breath. 'Is it?'

'So, what does that mean?' Glenys frowned.

'You are going to tell him, aren't you? You've got to, Joanna. It's his baby, too, remember?'

As if she could forget.

By the time she got back to London, Joanna was still in two minds. She knew she ought to tell Matt, but the last thing she wanted was for him to think she was only getting in touch with him again because she needed his support.

Of course, unless she dipped into the money her father had left her, she probably wouldn't be able to manage on her own. Childminders cost a small fortune these days. Her plans to use that money to accept David's invitation and become a partner in the gallery might have to be shelved.

Her mother believed Joanna had no choice but to tell Matt. She also reminded her that in a few months she wouldn't be able to work at all. Glenys suggested that when she left the gallery, she should move to Cornwall. She could stay with them until the baby was born.

'It will give you a breathing space,' she'd argued, when Joanna had demurred. 'I'm not asking you to move in with us permanently. But I don't like the idea of you having to cope with this alone.'

Joanna had left, assuring her that she'd do nothing without consulting her mother first, and re-alised how close she and Glenys had become since her father's death. The bitterness Angus had always felt towards his ex-wife had certainly influenced Joanna's teenage years.

David was glad to see her when she got back.

'This place hasn't been the same without you around,' he said, putting an arm around her shoulders and giving her a kiss on the cheek. 'I was half afraid you were having second thoughts about investing in the gallery. Are you sure Novak isn't still in the picture?'

'Hardly,' Joanna corrected him drily. 'As far as Matt is concerned, our marriage is over.'

'Well, you know how jealous I am,' said David good-humouredly. 'Anyway, I haven't forgotten he didn't exactly follow you back to England, did he? It's possible he's seeing someone else.'

But, remembering what Matt had said, Joanna found his comments rather irritating. 'You know it was nothing like that,' she said shortly. 'I told you his father had had another stroke. Matt's been dealing with the company in his absence.' She paused, and then added unwillingly, 'In any case, he's probably left the company by now. He's moving to the Bahamas—to write a book.'

'You're kidding.' David was incredulous, not

realising he was treading on dangerous ground. 'Perhaps he thinks if he tells you he's leaving NovCo, you won't fleece him for as much alimony, eh?'

Joanna resented his suggestion that Matt might cheat her. Yet wasn't that exactly what her father had said? She sighed, bending her head. 'I don't want any alimony,' she declared stiffly. 'Matt knows I can support myself.'

A sudden awareness of the baby and the problems it might create came into her mind. It was stupid, she knew, but she was dreading telling David. He apparently already thought she was gullible. He had yet to discover how gullible she'd been.

'You're crazy!' he said now, and for a moment Joanna was afraid she'd spoken her thoughts aloud. But when he continued, she soon realised she'd been mistaken. 'If I was in your shoes. I'd take him for every penny I could get.'

Needing confirmation of her condition, Joanna made an appointment with her doctor. And came out of the surgery with a handful of leaflets in her hands.

Okay, it was definite. She was expecting a baby. In the spring, Dr Foulds had told her. He would make an appointment in a few weeks for her to have her first scan at the local hospital, and they would be able to give her a date for when the baby was actually due.

Despite all her misgivings, Joanna found the prospect exciting. How ironic it was that she'd become pregnant now after only one night of love-making, when in the past she'd begun to believe she couldn't conceive.

She was having a baby. What was less certain was how Matt would feel about it. She'd finally decided that she had to tell him. Matt was the baby's father. It wouldn't be fair to keep it from him.

To that end, she waited until a time she could be reasonably sure he would be at the New York apartment. It was a little over a month since he'd visited London, but with Oliver still so ill, perhaps he might not have moved to the Bahamas quite yet.

She phoned in the early morning, New York time. Which meant she'd had to sneak out of the gallery so David didn't hear the call. She chose the little café where she often shopped for *cappuccinos* in the middle of the morning. Finding an empty booth, she ordered a diet soda, and made the call.

The phone seemed to ring for an unconscionable amount of time before it was answered. Joanna had been on the point of giving up, having decided that Matt had either left early for the office or he'd already sold the apartment.

Then the receiver was lifted and a languid female voice said, 'Do you know what time it is?'

Joanna swallowed convulsively, unable to think of anything to say. The woman's voice was not familiar and it was easy for her to think the worst. That Matt had taken a mistress, as David had said.

She was tempted to end the call, but she forced herself to speak. Swallowing again, she said, 'Is that you, Sophie? Is Matt there? I'd like to speak to him.'

The woman—*girl, whoever she was*—gave an impatient sigh. 'I'm not Sophie,' she said shortly. 'And Matt's not here. In any case, he wouldn't appreciate you calling him at this hour of the morning. Whatever it is, call him on his mobile. We usually find that's the safest thing to do.'

Joanna's mouth was unpleasantly dry, but she had to go on. 'I know the office number, but I don't know his mobile,' she admitted unwillingly.

The girl sighed again. 'If you give me your name, I'll tell him you called.'

'No.' All Joanna wanted to do now was end the call. 'No, it's not important. I—I'll catch him later.'

'Okay.' The woman sounded as if she didn't care one way or the other. Then, offhandedly, 'I don't know his mobile number either. But they might be willing to give it to you at the office.'

Joanna doubted it, but she said, 'Thanks,' and rang off. Annoyingly, she found she was shaking. She almost spilled the diet soda the girl brought for her, and, thrusting a five-pound note down on the table, she made her escape.

Outside, in the street, she couldn't prevent the hot tears that filled her eyes at the knowledge that someone else was staying in Matt's apartment. Someone who didn't know his mobile number, which was odd.

Was she just some female escort he'd brought home with him? Surely he hadn't had time to start a more permanent affair. But they were obviously sleeping together? Why else would a strange— *sleepy*—woman answer his phone at six o'clock in the morning?

She considered ringing again in the evening. But the thought of giving him her news, maybe in the presence of a new girlfriend, filled her with distaste. Remembering the angry way he'd left her apartment weeks ago, and now this morning's phone call, she was no longer sure what his reaction would be.

She sighed. Well, for the present, she would keep the baby's existence to herself. She would tell Matt, she assured herself. When she was ready. But he couldn't blame her for being secretive if he was keeping secrets of his own.

CHAPTER ELEVEN

MATT NOVAK SWUNG the tiller of his sleek racing dinghy towards the shore, and, ducking to avoid the boom, he guided the craft smoothly into the landing at Long Point.

It was still comparatively early in the morning. These days he found it difficult to sleep beyond six a.m., and in consequence he'd started taking the dinghy out before many of his fellow yachtsmen were on the water. Which suited him just fine.

While he was gradually adapting to the island lifestyle, he had no desire to get to know other expats like himself. He had come to the Bahamas to escape the corporate world. Not to make friends with the kind of people he'd left behind.

'You okay, Mr Matt?'

Henry Powell was waiting for him on the jetty and caught the rope that Matt threw to him, expertly fastening the craft to an iron mooring ring.

'I'm good,' Matt responded, checking that the

sail was secure before vaulting onto the landing. He raked back his unruly hair with a careless hand. 'Beautiful morning, Henry.'

'All mornings on Cable Cay are beautiful mornings,' declared Henry proudly.

He was an older man, of medium height and thick-set, his dark face leathery, lined from the sun. He and Matt had known one another since Matt was a boy, when his father had first brought him here on holiday all those years ago.

Oliver Novak had bought the villa at Long Point, but in recent years, he'd taken to renting it out during the winter months, with Henry acting as his steward. But Henry had been delighted when Matt had decided to buy the place from his father and occupy it on a more permanent basis.

Matt occasionally spent a week in New York, acting as his father's deputy, but since Sophie was making such a success of her tenure as CEO of NovCo, it was no longer such a necessary chore.

Henry paused now, and then added significantly, 'You ready to go up to the villa now, Mr Matt? 'Cos I have to tell you, you got a visitor.'

Matt stifled a curse and gave the older man a grim look. 'A visitor?' He could only think of his mother and he definitely did not want to see her.

'Yes, sir, Mr Matt.' Henry evidently sensed it

was not news his employer wanted to hear. 'It's Ms Sophie. She spent last night in Nassau and flew out here this morning.'

'Sophie?' Matt was both shocked and alarmed. He could think of no reason why Sophie might come all this way to see him unless something bad had happened to their father. Or to the company. 'Did she say why she was here?' he queried, and Henry shook his head. 'Does she look worried? Upset? What?'

Henry was thoughtful for a moment. 'She looks pretty much the way she always looks,' he decided cheerfully. 'I left her drinking coffee with Teresa.'

Matt checked the pockets of his shorts for his phone and briefly scanned the screen. No texts were screaming at him; no email messages begging to be read. So why the hell hadn't Sophie warned him she was coming? Unless she'd already guessed she wouldn't be welcome.

The landing where Matt was standing was just a few yards from the villa. Away to his left, one of the island's beautiful white sand beaches stretched away to a rocky promontory. To his right, the beach gave way to a thicket of mangroves clustered at the water's edge, which gave Long Point its complete privacy.

A little way beyond the mangroves was the small anchorage of Cable Bay, a favourite spot with the sailing fraternity. And not far from that was the small township of Cable Cay itself, and the tiny airport of Cable West.

Matt started towards the villa. He was surrounded by blossoming poinsettia, flowering hibiscus, and other colourful shrubs; vivid splashes of colour amid the palms that shielded the property from public view. That was one of the reasons why Oliver Novak had originally bought the villa. It was an oasis of privacy on what was a small, but fairly popular, island.

As Matt stalked up the crushed shell path to the villa, he endeavoured to find some comfort in the fact that had it been a matter of life and death, his mother would surely have let him know.

He found Sophie relaxing on the veranda that encircled the villa. A jug of coffee and two mugs were on the table in front of her, although Teresa had obviously returned to her duties.

Sophie had evidently packed for the weather in the islands. Her dark hair was casually caught up in a ponytail, and beige shorts and a floral halter top were definitely not the usual wear for January in New York.

'Hey,' she said, when she saw him, getting up as he climbed the steps to the veranda and bestowing a sisterly kiss on his stubbled cheek. 'Oh, you need a shave!'

Matt shrugged. 'I'm not going anywhere, am I?' He paused. 'How are things in New York?'

'Things are going great. As you know, if you remember how it was on your last visit.' Sophie sank back into her seat. 'We got the contract for the new exploration in the Arctic. And Andy Reichert thinks we might exceed all expectations this year.'

Matt pulled a wry face. 'Good for Andy.'

'You're not jealous, are you?'

Matt shook his head. 'I always thought he'd make a good CFO. Give him my congratulations and tell him in my opinion he's the best man for the job.'

Sophie snorted. 'I'm sure he'll appreciate that.'

'You're doing good, too, of course,' said Matt mildly, aware that Sophie could take offence very easily. 'But I can't believe you came here just to brag about your and Andy's success. What's going on? Dad and Mom are okay, aren't they?'

Sophie looked a little less confident now. 'Oh—sure,' she said. 'Dad has physio every day, and, although he'll never be the man he once was, he's gradually coming to terms with his limitations.' She paused. 'Mom's okay, too. I guess she's glad Dad's back home in Miami.'

'Right.' Matt tried to keep his impatience in check and with some tolerance, he said, 'So what is this? A break from routine? An impromptu holiday? If so, you should have let me—'

'Have you seen Joanna lately?'

Matt frowned. 'No.' He paused. 'Why would I? We're divorced, Sophie. You know that.'

'Has she been in touch?'

'No.' Matt was getting impatient. 'What is this, Sophie? Why are you asking me these questions?'

Sophie sighed. 'I just wondered if she'd phoned you, that's all. Do you think she'd have let you know if she was thinking of getting married again?'

Sophie's words hit Matt like a blow to his solar plexus. For a few moments, he could only stand there, gazing blankly at her, striving to breathe normally. Then he sought one of the cushioned bamboo chairs at the other side of the table and dragged himself into it.

Sophie looked anxious now, and when Henry appeared from the back of the villa, she said swiftly, 'Will you get some brandy for Mr Matt? He—he's not feeling well.'

'Sure thing,' began the old man, but Matt stopped him.

'No brandy, Henry. Coffee will do.'

When they were alone again, Matt sucked in a grim breath. 'Who told you she's getting married again?'

'No one.' Sophie looked uncomfortable now. 'I just thought she might be.'

'And why would you think that? Have you spoken to Joanna?'

Sophie shrugged. 'Well, I have seen her.' She paused. 'But I haven't spoken to her.'

'So this is all supposition?'

'Sort of.'

'What do you mean—sort of?'

Sophie looked unhappy now. 'It's not up to me to tell you what's going on. I came here with the best of intentions. I can't help it if you don't like my news.'

Matt shook his head. 'What Joanna does or doesn't do is no concern of mine any more,' he reminded her. 'Okay, I agree, she might have let me know if she was thinking of getting married again. But it's really nothing to do with me.' He paused. 'Where did this come from anyway? The London office?'

'Well, I was in London,' Sophie agreed reluctantly. 'Actually, I'd decided to look her up.' Sophie hesitated. 'I went to the gallery. A week ago.'

Matt scowled. 'So why didn't you speak to her?'

'I—I intended to, obviously.' She paused and then continued, 'I'd got a taxi to the gallery. It was a spur of the moment thing, and I was about to get out of the cab when I saw her. But she wasn't alone. She was—she was with another man. They were really—you know—cosy with one another. He—kissed her, actually. So I just asked the driver to take me back to Oxford Street.'

Matt stifled a curse. Bellamy, he thought grimly. The other man had just been waiting for their divorce to be made final before making his move. Matt didn't really know why he cared. Dammit, why couldn't Sophie have kept this information to herself?

His scowl deepening, he said, 'And you really expect me to go and see her?' He shook his head. 'Why?'

'I think she might like to see you, that's all.'

Matt's mouth compressed. 'That doesn't make sense.'

'Probably not.' Sophie shrugged as if getting tired of the argument.

Matt gave her a brooding look. Joanna had always insisted that she and Bellamy were friends. Yet foolish as it was, he couldn't bear the thought of her with anyone else.

Damn her!

His scowl deepened. 'So do you think I'm harbouring some desperate wish to see her again?'

'Aren't you?' Sophie was annoyingly direct.

Matt's jaw hardened. 'You should have got out of the cab and asked her what was going on instead of bringing this to me.'

Sophie groaned. 'But I wouldn't have known what to say.'

'And you think I would?'

Matt's hands curled into fists on the table. But fortunately, Henry appeared at that moment with a fresh pot of coffee, sugar, cream and two cups, and set his burden carefully in front of Sophie.

'Will you...?' he began and Sophie nodded.

'Leave it to me, Henry,' she said, with a grateful smile. 'Thank you.'

She poured two cups, leaving Matt's black but adding two sugars before pushing the cup towards him. 'Go on,' she said. 'Drink it. You look as if you need it.'

Matt's lips twisted. 'Do I?' His tone was gruff. 'Sophie, I haven't seen Joanna in—what? Five months?'

'But you did go to London to see her after our father's stroke, didn't you? I thought maybe you and she had mended your differences or something.'

Matt shrugged. 'Hardly that.'

'But you took her back to the hotel when she was in Miami.' Sophie hesitated. 'Did you sleep with her?'

Matt took the coffee she'd poured him and swallowed a mouthful before replying, 'What's that got to do with you?'

Sophie stared at him incredulously. 'You were with her when I called the hotel to tell you about our father, weren't you? Was she the reason why you didn't answer your phone? My God, Matt, I thought you had more sense than that.'

Not that it mattered now, but Matt had thought so, too.

CHAPTER TWELVE

JOANNA CARRIED THE cup of tea she'd just made for herself through to the front office. She didn't drink coffee these days, and, truth to tell, she hadn't missed it.

All the same, she didn't mind admitting she was tired, even though it was barely four o'clock in the afternoon. Getting up at half-past seven in the morning to arrive at the gallery before nine o'clock had begun to take its toll.

Still, she consoled herself, she only had two more days to go before she left to have the baby. Well, not exactly to *have* the baby, she corrected herself. But she was over six months now and she'd finally given in and accepted her mother's invitation to spend the latter weeks of her pregnancy in Padsworth.

What happened after the baby was born was another matter. All she knew for sure was that during the course of the pregnancy, she had become attached to the small life growing inside her. He had become a part of her. The fact that he was a part of Matt, too, was something she still had to deal with.

Sitting down, she ran her hand over the bump that swelled her jersey shift. She felt the kick that pushed against her palm and couldn't prevent a smile. Evidently her son wasn't tired, she acknowledged. Even though his energetic antics had kept her awake half the night.

Not for the first time in recent weeks, she thought about her ex-husband and what he was doing now. The fact that he knew nothing about his son's existence had begun to play on her mind. But she would tell him, she assured herself. She was only putting it off until the baby was born.

To begin with, she'd felt justified in not calling him again. She didn't want to embarrass him, she told herself. And she certainly didn't want anyone to feel sorry for her. This woman he was with: who knew how serious that was? After the way he'd walked out of her apartment, she'd had no reason to believe he would be glad to hear from her again.

But as the weeks went by and the baby grew inside her, she knew she'd been fooling herself. Of course, he'd want to know about the baby. The trouble was, she had no idea how she could approach him now. She should have phoned again when she'd had the chance, she thought unhappily. Matt might not care about her, but she was sure he'd care about the baby.

The fact that he hadn't challenged her petition for divorce was some justification, surely. Apparently, the fact that there might have been consequences from the night they'd slept together hadn't occurred to him. But why would they? she'd mused ruefully. They'd been trying for a baby for so many years without any success.

No, after that confrontation in London, he appeared to have washed his hands of her. And she consoled herself with the thought that there'd be time enough to think about how she was going to handle the situation after the baby was born. The last communication she'd had from his solicitor had quoted the address on Cable Cay that Matt had given her. So, evidently, he'd left NovCo now and moved to the Bahamas, as he'd planned.

Alone?

Pushing that thought aside, Joanna studied the details of the showing that was taking place the following week on the website. Since becoming a partner in the business, she'd set up the website and acquired a list of email addresses she could use to announce forthcoming events. It had worked well and drawn a lot of new people into the gallery, people who only learned about things through social media.

The young artist being featured this coming week was a favourite of hers, and she hoped the exhibition went well. Unfortunately—or fortunately, whichever way you looked at it—Joanna would not be around to see it. She was leaving for Cornwall on Saturday, much against David's better judgement, she had to admit.

He believed she'd be better off staying in London. He'd be on hand if she needed him, and she could always continue updating the website from home. These days, he deferred more and more to her judgement, and there was no doubt that she would miss the excitement of not knowing what each day was going to bring.

Despite learning how expensive a childminder was going to be, she'd still been able to invest in the gallery, which she hoped would provide security for the future. Initially, she'd believed she could only afford one or the other. But because when she and Matt had divorced, she'd been contacted by Matt's solicitor with a view to selling her shares in NovCo, she'd decided she owed it to her father to accept the interest they'd made.

As she sipped her tea, she heard the outer door

open and guessed her partner was back from lunch. David had been schmoozing with a wealthy collector, who he hoped would agree to attend the following week's showing.

She heard footsteps in the gallery, but David didn't immediately come through to the office. Either he was making adjustments to the display or it wasn't David at all. Which meant she should show her face. It wouldn't do to allow a would-be customer to feel neglected.

Setting down her tea, she rose to her feet, briefly checking her reflection in the glass of a picture hung above David's desk. She wore her hair in a single braid these days and, apart from a few errant strands curling about her ears, it hung smoothly over one shoulder.

But it was almost the end of the day and any make-up she'd started out with was virtually non-existent. Not that a touch of mascara and a smear of cinnamon lip gloss achieved much. All the same, with her prominent bump, she bore little resemblance to the glamorous receptionists she'd seen in other galleries around town.

Stepping out into the gallery proper, she glanced quickly about her. Had she been mistaken? There didn't appear to be anybody about. But the gallery was quite big, and the stone bases supporting the current display of bronzes blocked her view.

'Hello,' she called, hoping someone would answer. 'Can I help you?'

'I hope so.'

The voice was sardonic but, in spite of the passage of time, so recognisable that Joanna's breath caught helplessly in the back of her throat.

Matt, she saw with some dismay, stepped out from behind the wooden frame that stood at the front of the gallery, announcing the current artist's identity. In narrow-fitting jeans and a thigh-length leather jacket, the collar tipped up against the rain, he looked heartbreakingly familiar, and she found it hard to tear her eyes away.

Licking her dry lips, she said, 'Matt.' She took a breath. 'What are you doing here?'

'Do you need to ask?'

Looking at Joanna now, Matt was glad he'd had the sense to check out the gallery before actually speaking to her.

Despite what Sophie had said, he hadn't intended to make this trip, but something—some suspicion, perhaps, that Sophie hadn't been entirely honest with him—had compelled him to find out for himself. He'd arrived in London late the previous day—much against his better judgement, it was true—and as soon as he'd checked into his hotel, he'd had his chauffeur bring him here.

It was January and it had been fairly dark when he'd arrived at the gallery and, as it happened, Joanna had just been leaving for the day. She'd been alone, a long wraparound coat attempting to conceal her appearance, but Matt had known at once what it was Sophie had been trying so hard not to say.

Joanna was pregnant. And fairly well advanced if he didn't miss his guess. But how well advanced and whose baby was it? He had a right to be suspicious, when not only had she not told him, but she knew as well as he did how singularly unsuccessful in their efforts to get pregnant they had been.

He hadn't attempted to speak to her then. He couldn't.

He'd had Jack drive him back to his hotel and had spent the rest of the evening getting mindlessly drunk, trying to erase the image of his wife in bed with another man.

This morning, he'd phoned Sophie, uncaring that it had been the middle of the night in New York, and expunged a little of his frustration on her. 'Why the hell didn't you tell me?' He'd practically yelled the words. 'I'd at least have been warned what to expect.'

He'd felt guilty later, and he'd phoned again and apologised for blaming her. But, God Almighty, what had he done to deserve this? he wondered. And why the hell hadn't Joanna told him herself?

Though why should she, he argued, if it wasn't his baby? He might be beating himself up unnecessarily over an event that had nothing to do with him. On top of which, he had the mother of all headaches, a combination of a hangover and the bitter recriminations that had kept him awake half the night.

Now he moved forward. 'Well, let me see,' he said, answering her question, and there wasn't an atom of warmth in his voice. 'I thought you might have something you wanted to tell me.' His eyes swept insolently down her body, lingering with undisguised contempt on the bump that swelled her dress. 'Ah, I see you do.'

The more charitable thoughts Joanna had been having about her ex-husband vanished with his words. His arrogance infuriated her.

'Why should you presume I have anything to tell you?' she demanded, forgetting all about the feelings of guilt she had been nurturing earlier.

Her hand slid protectively over her belly. 'I don't believe I've made any claim against you.'

Matt's eyes turned hostile. Suddenly, despite what he'd been thinking, he knew the baby was his. Joanna had never been much good at lying, and he could see the apprehension in her eyes.

'Just when were you planning on telling me?' he demanded, ignoring the unexpected thrill of anticipation. 'I hate to remind you, but I do have some rights where this baby is concerned.'

Somehow Joanna found the words to defend herself. Which wasn't easy when Matt was gazing at her with contempt in his eyes. His jaw had hardened and, in spite of everything, she couldn't look away from him. He looked so good, she thought resentfully. His skin was deeply tanned, evidence of his change of occupation, and he'd had his hair cut shorter, exposing the strong column of his neck. Evidently, he'd been enjoying life; apparently unaware that once again he had radically changed hers.

'I believe you'll find that in the UK, the mother has parental rights over the father,' she said stiffly, not realising she was virtually admitting the baby was his.

Matt's hands curled into fists in the pockets of his jacket. She was so bloody smug, he thought angrily. Talking to him about rights when she hadn't even had the decency to tell him she was pregnant. Because if he'd had any lingering doubts about its parentage, she'd just removed them.

Sucking in a breath, he shrugged. 'Okay,' he said. 'I'll just wait until the child is born and I can prove that I'm the father. I believe there are Parental Responsibility Orders issued by your courts that might—'

Joanna held up a hand. 'All right, all right,' she broke in unsteadily. 'It's your baby. I'm not denying it.'

'So why wasn't I told?' Matt asked.

'I—' Joanna hesitated, not wanting to continue but knowing she had to. 'I tried. I rang your New York apartment early one morning, as soon as I knew for certain that I was pregnant. Some— some woman answered.'

'What woman?' Matt scowled. 'Did you get her name?'

'No, I didn't get her name.' Joanna gasped. 'My God, have there been so many women staying in your apartment that you don't even know who it was?'

'Of course not.' Matt expelled a weary breath. 'It was probably Andy Reichert's wife. He and his family are living in the apartment at present.'

He hesitated. 'Or it could have been his daughter, I suppose.'

Joanna felt her face burning with unwelcome colour. 'Well—well, I didn't know that, did I? Anyway, whoever it was, she said you weren't there. That I should ring back later.'

'Did you give her your name?'

'No.' Joanna sighed.

'Did you ring back later?'

'No.' Joanna bit her lip. 'I was—upset. I really thought that—'

'Yes, I can guess what you thought.' Matt was finding it difficult to keep his temper. 'How do you think I felt when my own sister had to give me some clue as to what was going on?'

'Sophie?' Joanna frowned. 'So how did she find out?'

'She saw you. She was working in London and thought she'd look you up.'

'But she didn't.'

'Oh, she did, but you didn't see her. Sophie has some discretion.' He shook his head incredulously. 'For God's sake, Joanna, what could she have said to you?'

'I don't know.' Joanna was on edge. 'Maybe I'd have welcomed her advice.'

'Her advice!'

Matt tamped down his anger with an effort. She knew better than anyone that they'd tried for years to have a baby. And now, when it had happened, she'd kept the news to herself, because she'd apparently believed he was having an affair.

If she hadn't killed any feelings he might have had for her months ago, she'd certainly done a good job now. Yet he couldn't deny her condition suited her. There was a quality about her, that famous pregnancy glow, he supposed, that surrounded her. She was wearing her hair longer, too, and the braid she wore curled sensuously about her breast.

He wondered if she was seeing anyone. Just because she was pregnant didn't mean there wasn't a man hanging around. Some men were attracted to pregnant women. And despite his own feelings towards her, he didn't like the thought of another man in her bed.

Which was stupid, he chided himself. It wasn't as if he'd been entirely celibate since their divorce. Okay, there'd only been that one occasion when he'd submitted to taking another woman to bed. But the fact was, although she'd been more than willing, he'd left without consummating the affair.

'So what now?' Matt asked tersely. 'I'm assuming from your words that you've had some thoughts about the future.'

Joanna hesitated. 'I'm keeping the baby, if that's what you're asking.'

'It wasn't. I would have thought that was a given.' Matt frowned. 'So, surely you aren't planning on working until the baby is born. Dammit, Joanna, use some of the money I've deposited to your account in the past and give yourself a break.'

Joanna swallowed. Should she tell him she was going to stay with her mother and Lionel? And if she did, would he insist on speaking to them, too? The alternative was letting him think she was going to go on working, and who knew if he'd turn up again when she wasn't here?

'Well, I—' she was beginning, when the outer door opened again and David breezed into the gallery.

He was obviously in a good mood; his face was flushed and she guessed he'd been successful in securing support for the exhibition. Not to mention a few gin and tonics over lunch, which accounted for his florid appearance.

His good humour vanished when he saw Matt, however.

'Joanna?' he said, the uncertainty evident in his tone. 'I didn't know you were expecting a visitor.'

'I surprised her.' Matt's words overrode any attempt she might have made to explain. 'As I was in England, I thought I'd check up on Joanna's condition. It's not every day your ex-wife finds she's pregnant with your child *after* the divorce.'

David gave her a horrified look. 'It's *his* baby!' he exclaimed, and Joanna wanted to groan in frustration. She'd deliberately not told David who the father was, letting him think it was someone she'd met after she'd returned from Miami.

Matt, meanwhile, was smiling smugly. 'Of course it's my baby,' he said. 'Why else do you think I'm here?'

Joanna schooled her features. Why was she surprised? All he was really interested in was claiming his child.

How naïve she'd been in thinking he might care about her.

'So how long has he been here?' David interrupted her unhappy train of thought with a question of his own. 'He's not going down to Cornwall with you, is he?'

CHAPTER THIRTEEN

So MUCH FOR keeping her plans to herself, thought Joanna resignedly. For heaven's sake, why couldn't David have kept his mouth shut?

'Of course not,' she said now. 'I had no idea Matt was in the country until he turned up. Why on earth would you think I'd ask him to do such a thing?'

'Oh, I don't know.' David regarded the other man coldly. 'As he's the baby's father, he probably thinks he has some rights.'

'I do have some rights.' Matt regarded him with equal contempt. 'And now would you mind giving us a little privacy?'

David was belligerent. 'If Joanna had wanted to see you, she'd have told me.'

'Would she?' Matt looked enquiringly at Joanna. 'She apparently kept the baby's father's identity a secret.'

'Probably because she was ashamed of getting involved with you again,' retorted David angrily.

He turned to Joanna. 'Would you like me to throw him out?'

'You're singularly lacking in imagination if you think you could do such a thing,' drawled Matt drily. 'Give it up, Bellamy. This is one occasion when your doubtful talents are not needed.'

'You can't speak to me like that.'

'I think I just did.'

'Oh, please,' Joanna said, addressing her remarks to no one in particular. It concerned her that David's face was much redder now and she was afraid his blood pressure was rising. 'Can we just calm down?'

Thankfully, her ex-husband chose not to pursue the subject and instead turned to Joanna. 'Am I to understand that you're planning to spend the remaining months of your pregnancy in Padsworth?' he enquired coolly, and Joanna put both hands on the small of her back in an effort to relieve the ache in her spine.

She looked tired, thought Matt, realising that she probably spent a considerable part of the day on her feet. But he was fairly sure she wouldn't welcome any sympathy.

'Possibly,' she said, not wanting to admit it, and David chose that moment to intervene again.

'You have no part in this, Novak. Why don't you take the hint and get lost?'

Matt ignored him, and Joanna was grateful. Her ex-husband could be dangerous when crossed, and she wished David would just keep his opinions to himself. It was hard enough dealing with Matt, knowing how he felt about her, without having to cope with the other man's well-meant interference as well.

Matt had evidently come to the same conclusion. 'I think we need to talk. Privately,' he said, echoing her sentiments.

'We can go to my hotel, if you like, or there's a coffee bar a couple of blocks down the street that looks okay.'

'All right,' she said, avoiding David's outraged expression. 'I'll get my coat.'

'You don't have to go with him,' Bellamy began, following her into the office, and she shook her head.

'It's better this way,' she said, slipping her arms into the sleeves of her heather-coloured tweed duster. 'And actually, I was thinking of leaving early today. It's such a horrible afternoon, I doubt anyone else is going to turn up.'

David looked sulky. 'I wanted to tell you about

my lunch with Theo Konstantinos,' he protested, but Joanna could only shake her head.

'I'll hear all about it in the morning,' she promised, wrapping her coat about her. 'See you tomorrow.'

A sleek black chauffeur-driven limousine was idling at the kerb outside, clearly in breach of the *No Parking* zone that operated outside the gallery.

But Joanna had no desire to get into a car with Matt.

'It's just a few yards to the café,' she said, starting along the pavement. 'If that's your driver, I'd advise him to move on. The police are pretty vigilant around here.'

Matt scowled. She was probably right, of course, but it was a bloody awful afternoon. He was used to sunshine, to temperatures in the eighties. Even walking maybe a quarter mile in this downpour seemed crazy.

But abandoning any alterative, he stopped at the car and told his driver he'd call him when he wanted picking up. Then he strode after Joanna, amazed that she was still wearing high heels despite her condition.

The coffee shop was crowded. Joanna guessed that a lot of its customers had come inside to shelter from the rain. In consequence, the only seats available were at the counter, tall stools that she had great difficulty in climbing onto at present.

Matt regarded her doubtfully. 'Do you need a hand?' he asked, and she gave him an old-fashioned look.

'I'm pregnant, Matt. Not senile. It's better than standing, believe me.'

He did believe her. He wouldn't have been able to stand in those heels. Sliding onto the stool beside her, he steadied himself with his hand on the counter, and his arm inadvertently brushed against her bump. Through the folds of her coat, her belly felt firmer than he'd imagined; solid. Somehow, he'd expected it to be soft and pliable, but it wasn't.

He realised he wanted to touch her again, to possibly feel a kick from the little person growing inside her. Dear God, it was his child. That reality put everything else into raw perspective.

Matt ordered a coffee for himself, but Joanna said she would just have a diet soda. 'Do you want a muffin with that?' he asked, and she gave a reluctant smile.

'Don't you think I look fat enough?' she countered humorously. 'No, the soda is fine for me. But if you're hungry—'

'I'm not.' Matt wondered if he'd ever feel hungry again.

'And you're not fat,' he assured her. 'Just—pregnant, that's all.'

And how incredible was that? Dear God, it was going to take time to get used to the idea.

Meanwhile, Joanna was wondering if he was as nervous as she was. But, no. Matt Novak didn't do 'nervous'. Not in her experience anyway. But his lean face did look a little paler than it had done when he'd first walked into the gallery, and she guessed he hadn't really believed that she was pregnant until then.

Deciding to take the initiative, she said, 'So what did Sophie say to bring you to London?'

Matt arched a rueful brow as the waiter brought their drinks. 'Oh, she asked me if I knew if you were getting married again.'

'Married?' Joanna looked puzzled and Matt was relieved.

'I guess it was the only way she knew to get my interest,' he said drily. 'She couldn't be sure I'd do anything about it, but she took that chance.'

Joanna nodded. 'Knowing what a control freak you are, I suppose she knew you'd resent me doing anything without your knowledge,' she remarked, pulling her soda towards her.

'I'll ignore that and just say, I was concerned about you,' he retorted. 'And I have to admit, the thought that you might be marrying Bellamy wasn't a good one.'

Joanna sighed. If only he knew. Changing the subject a little, she said, 'Did Sophie know we'd slept together?'

'Not initially, no.'

'But you told her?'

'She asked,' said Matt flatly, sprinkling sugar into his coffee.

'But she didn't tell you I was pregnant?'

'No. As I say, Sophie is discreet. Or she can be in certain circumstances.'

'So your mother doesn't know you've come to England?'

'Need you ask?' Matt took a mouthful of his coffee, wiping his lip with the back of his hand. 'What with my father demanding so much attention, she hasn't had the time to check up on me.'

'Oh, God, Oliver, yes.' Joanna was ashamed she hadn't asked about his father before. 'How is he? I've thought about him a lot since you told me about his stroke. Has he made a good recovery?'

'He'll get there if he stops arguing with the physios,' replied Matt, pulling a wry face. 'He's accepted that he won't be fit enough to work again, but he can be a pretty difficult patient at times. He'll never recover the use of his left arm, unfortunately, but, as we keep telling him, that's a small price to pay for his being alive.'

Joanna nodded. 'If—*when*—you see him again, give him my best, won't you?'

'I will.' Then, after a moment, 'So, how have you been?'

'Not too bad.' Joanna sipped her soda. 'I had some morning sickness to start with, but that's normal. And during the last few weeks, I've been feeling pretty tired by the end of the day. But that's normal, too. I'm usually in bed by ten.'

Realising she was chattering, Joanna bit her tongue. Matt wasn't interested in the everyday details of each trimester. He'd meant how was she feeling now? But his response was typical.

'You shouldn't still be working,' he said. 'Particularly not for that—for Bellamy.'

'David's been really kind to me.' She hesitated. 'In any case, I don't actually work *for* him anymore. I used some of the money you sent after selling my shares in NovCo and became his partner.'

'You're kidding!' Matt was appalled. 'So what happens next? You get married and share everything?'

'Oh, Matt.' She shook her head. 'You couldn't be more wrong where David is concerned.' She bit her lip and then added, much against her better judgement, 'He's more likely to be interested in you than in me!'

Matt was stunned. 'I can't believe it.'

'No, well, it's David's business, not mine. FYI, he has a partner. They've been together for—oh, I don't know—about five years.'

Matt absorbed what she'd said with relief and incredulity. Relief, because it meant his fears so far as David and Joanna were concerned were groundless, and incredulity because David had always seemed to treat her as a man treated the woman he loved.

And perhaps he did love her. Whatever the situation, Matt owed the man an apology. An apology he could never give, he realised, not without betraying Joanna's trust.

Joanna took a deep breath now. 'Anyway, as you heard, I'm taking a temporary leave of absence at the end of this week.'

'To go stay with your mother?' Matt regarded her closely. 'Is that what you really want?'

Joanna shrugged. 'It was her idea,' she said defensively, tracing a pattern on the counter with her fingernail.

She hesitated and then added, 'I should tell you, she didn't approve of me keeping the baby's existence to myself. When I first saw you, I thought she'd contacted you.'

Matt hesitated, and then said, 'So how do you feel about spending the next couple months in Cornwall?'

'Well...' Joanna sighed and Matt waited somewhat curiously for her reply. 'I can't go on working at the gallery, and she and Lionel have been very good to me,' she added, jiggling the straw in her glass.

Matt realised that she'd probably thought it was a good solution. But that was before he'd been involved. This was his child she was carrying, he thought possessively. He should have some say in where she spent the rest of her pregnancy.

'I saw from your solicitor's letter that you're living in the Bahamas these days,' she said, probably hoping to divert him, but she'd inadvertently given him an idea.

'I told you I was going to buy a couple of businesses on Cable Cay,' said Matt casually. 'I guess you could say I'm helping to bolster the tourist trade on the island. And I've done some writing, too. Not the great American novel,' he added, as her eyes widened. 'Just a couple of articles for the local rag.'

Joanna was impressed. 'And does it keep you busy?'

'Well, that and some sailing,' agreed Matt, wanting to get back to the real reason he'd brought it up. He paused. 'When is the baby due?'

Joanna hesitated, and he wondered if she was thinking of lying to him. But she evidently thought better of it, and replied quietly, 'Around the middle of March. The second week, I think they said.'

'Do you have a date?'

Matt regarded her enquiringly, his arm brushing her sleeve as he reached for his coffee, and Joanna felt her awareness of him rocket up a notch. Hormones, she reminded herself again, drawing away from him. One of the women at the clinic she attended had been talking about how sexy she was finding her husband these days. A crazy admission, but Joanna couldn't say her reactions where Matt was concerned were all that different.

Now she said shortly, 'Really, Matt, what does it matter? I doubt if you'll be around when he's born.'

'He?' Matt was instantly distracted, picking up on that before anything else. 'You're having a

boy? For God's sake, Joanna, were you going to deprive me of seeing my own son?'

Joanna's face burned. Matt had spoken thoughtlessly, and his voice had been much too loud. She doubted anyone in their immediate vicinity hadn't heard that damning accusation.

Eyes turned in their direction; curious eyes, eyes that held a certain amount of sympathy—for him. She wondered if she'd ever be able to come into this coffee shop again without being recognised, or meeting someone's censorious gaze.

'I want to go,' she said abruptly, sliding off her stool, and draping the strap of her bag over one shoulder. 'Thanks for the drink.'

'Wait!'

But Joanna wasn't listening to him. With her head down, she headed for the exit. Let Matt deal with the fallout, she thought resentfully. He'd created it. All she wanted to do was go home and lock herself in her apartment.

And give way to the tears that were threatening to destroy what little confidence she had left.

CHAPTER FOURTEEN

JOANNA WASN'T SURPRISED when Matt followed her out of the coffee shop. She doubted if even he was prepared to face the sympathy of the customers. For herself, she wished ardently that she'd brought her car this morning. It would have been so much easier to slide behind the wheel of her little Mini and make her getaway.

But these days, she used a bus to take her to and from the gallery. Using her car meant she had to find a parking space, and often that meant a seriously long walk to the gallery. Something she preferred not to do in her present condition.

It was certainly not a day for hanging around. The rain was coming down in sheets. A glance at her watch informed her that the next bus wasn't due for another fifteen minutes. And there wasn't even a bus shelter to offer some protection.

Dammit!

Now Matt would offer her a lift, something she had hoped to avoid. Okay, she accepted that he was probably not going to be satisfied until he knew every minute detail of her plans. But being alone with him, talking about their son, meant she was admitting him back into her life.

Yet did she have a choice?

Joanna swallowed a little convulsively. When had she started thinking of the baby as *their* son?

'Where the hell are you going?'

Predictably, Matt had caught up to her and he grabbed her sleeve as she hurried along the pavement, bringing her to a standstill. Strong fingers sent bolts of fire up her arm, and, controlling her unwelcome reaction, Joanna turned to give him an indignant look. 'I'm going home,' she said, aware that she sounded defensive. 'Where else?'

Matt seethed. 'Where did you park your car?'

'I didn't.' Realising that he probably wouldn't believe her, Joanna sighed. 'I generally use the bus,' she appended, watching as Matt fished his mobile phone out of his pocket. 'There's never anywhere to park around here.'

'Is that so?' Matt flicked open the phone, punched one of the keys and then spoke into the mouthpiece. 'Now, Jack,' he said without preamble, and closed the phone again.

Joanna's shoulders sagged. 'Look, I know this

meeting hasn't been very satisfactory—' she began, and Matt gave her an ironic look.

'You think?'

'But it's a bit early to be discussing what's going to happen after the baby's born.' She paused. 'Don't you think?'

'Dear Lord, I'm still getting used to the idea that you're having a baby,' said Matt harshly. 'And now I hear you're having it in less than three months.' He shook his head. 'I want to know everything about it. And that definitely includes where the baby is born.'

Joanna sighed. She was getting wet and, with an effort, she pulled her arm away.

'Come on, Joanna.' There was no humour in his voice. 'I'm not leaving here without you. We can go to your apartment, or my hotel. It's up to you.'

Joanna bit her lip, and then, shrugging her shoulders, she allowed him to help her into the back of the limousine that cruised to a stop beside them. There was no point in quarrelling with Matt. Not when she had no defence.

'Your apartment?' suggested Matt, sliding in beside her, and she was immediately made aware of his masculinity.

The mixture of aftershave and the clean male smell of his body drifted over her. This was why she'd wished she'd brought her own car. In the confines of the back seat of the limousine, Matt was far too close for comfort. Far too close for her shattered nerves to ignore.

Aware that he was waiting for her response, she glanced at him out of the corners of her eyes. 'No. Your hotel,' she said firmly, guessing he would not be expecting that. 'Is it still the Savoy? We can have afternoon tea in the foyer.'

Matt's mouth compressed. 'I'm staying at a small hotel in Knightsbridge, actually,' he responded after a moment. 'But we can have afternoon tea in my suite, if you like.'

Afternoon tea in his suite!

Not likely.

Joanna's lips parted. 'I—well, perhaps you'd better come to the apartment, then,' she said, as he'd probably anticipated she would. 'But the place is a mess. I've been sorting things out for the past couple of weeks and there are boxes everywhere.'

Matt shrugged and leant forward to give Jack Dougherty his instructions. Then there was an oppressive silence until the chauffeur drew into the grounds of Colgate Court.

The place looked even less attractive in the rain, Matt thought morosely as he followed Joanna into the building. But at least there was no grim-faced caretaker waiting to block their way.

She hadn't been exaggerating about the state of the apartment. There were suitcases in the foyer and clothes and books all over the living-room floor. Which was another source of irritation. If Matt had delayed his trip to London, she might well have left this address. Would he have guessed where she'd gone, or might he have had to go to the gallery and tackle Bellamy? Not a prospect he'd have viewed with any degree of enthusiasm before today, he admitted wryly.

Matt's hands curled into fists in his pockets. Thank God, she was leaving here anyway. The room was cold, and he guessed she'd turned off the heating while she was at work. Why did she insist on economising when she had a healthy bank balance? It was ridiculous, and he was feeling bloody frustrated by the whole affair.

'Do you want some tea?'

Tea?

No, Matt didn't want any tea. He wouldn't have said no to a glass of whisky, but he doubted Joanna kept anything like that here.

Joanna had shed her coat and was presently filling the kettle at the small sink. Matt's eyes were irresistibly drawn to her body but he shook his head impatiently and looked away.

There was little to see beyond the windows as he'd observed the last time he was here. This whole place was a dump, he thought, uncharitably. And possibly damp, too. He was glad Joanna wasn't planning on having the baby here, even if the prospect of her moving to Cornwall was only slightly less acceptable.

'I don't have any coffee to offer you,' Joanna was continuing, and, turning towards her, Matt noticed that the hand taking a cup from one of the virtually empty cupboards beside her was shaking.

It was difficult for him not to feel sympathetic towards her then. This was the woman he had loved for over six years. He didn't want to have any feelings for her but, whether it was just a physical thing or not, his body was humming with an unwelcome awareness of her nearness.

He swore, forcing such thoughts aside. He had to concentrate on the present and what he was going to do now.

While the kettle boiled, Joanna came into the living area and gestured towards the easy chair beside the windows. 'Why don't you sit down? I won't be a minute.'

Matt frowned. 'Why? Where are you going?'

Joanna made an embarrassed gesture. 'I'm going to the bathroom,' she said awkwardly. 'It's a hazard of my condition, I'm afraid.'

'Ah.'

Matt acknowledged the problem and Joanna hurried out of the room. But when she returned, he was still standing in the middle of the floor, and although he'd loosened his leather coat, it still hung damply from his shoulders.

There were drops of rain sparkling on his dark hair, and she recalled how she used to grip handfuls of his hair when he was making love to her. She remembered winding her legs about his hips, emitting muffled cries of satisfaction every time she reached another climax. And then, lying indolently beneath him, content to feel him inside her, prolonging the visceral connection for as long as she possibly could.

Oh, God!

Joanna stifled a groan, wondering when she was going to stop having these—what? *Erotic* thoughts about Matt? She could blame it on the pregnancy, but she had the feeling that they weren't going to go away any time soon.

The kettle had boiled in her absence, and as she crossed the room she was intensely conscious of

Matt's eyes assessing her appearance. Desperate to distract him, she asked again if he would like a cup of tea, anything to make this situation less fraught than it seemed, but Matt merely shook his head.

'No, thanks,' he said, crossing the living room towards her. He paused in the entry to the kitchen annexe, successfully blocking her exit. 'Is there any chance that you could just sit down and talk to me?'

'Oh—sure.'

Joanna managed a quick acknowledgement, adding hot water to the teabag she'd placed in her cup. She opened the fridge and took a carton of milk from the door. Then, when Matt was on the point of demanding that she stop fussing around, she added a little milk to her cup and came towards him.

'Excuse me,' she said, indicating that he was in her way, and Matt gritted his teeth and moved aside.

Joanna carried her cup over to the sofa, and seated herself on the edge of the cushions. Then, cradling the hot cup between her icy palms, she said, 'You should sit down, too.'

Matt dragged one of the dining chairs over to the sofa and, swinging it around, he straddled it, facing her. He'd had time to think about what he was going to say, and Joanna was slightly disturbed by his grim expression.

He was ominously silent for a moment. And then, he said quietly, 'I don't want you to spend the rest of your pregnancy in Padsworth.'

Joanna was taken aback. She'd half expected him to join her on the sofa, but he hadn't. This was a very different Matt from the man she'd slept with in Miami, she thought uneasily.

Gathering her small store of composure, Joanna sipped her tea, to avoid meeting those intent dark eyes. 'Well, I don't want to stay here,' she said at last.

Matt considered her flushed face with some impatience. 'I don't want you to stay here either.'

'So you understand why I'm going to Cornwall?'

'I understand you thought it was your only option,' Matt agreed tersely. 'If you'd told me the truth from the beginning, we wouldn't be having this discussion. I'd have offered you an alternative.'

'What alternative?' Joanna still had some pride. 'I don't need your support, Matt.'

'Maybe not, but you're going to get it,' he retorted. He controlled his temper with an effort.

'God, I still can't believe you kept this from me for so long.'

'Must we go over that again?' Joanna sighed. 'There was always the possibility that you might deny the child was yours.'

'You think?'

'All right.' She lifted a careless hand. 'I don't think you would have done that. I'm sorry. I should have told you.' She paused. 'Are you happy now?'

Matt's jaw hardened. 'Where do you plan to have this baby?' His voice was tense. 'I don't want you going into labour in some remote village in Cornwall. There's no maternity hospital in the village, I know that, and it's the middle of winter. If anything goes wrong, how long before you can get expert help?'

'Why would you think that anything might go wrong?'

'Joanna, we've been trying to have a baby for a few years now. Do you want to take the chance that there might be a complication?'

'Well, it won't be the middle of winter when I have the baby,' she replied reasonably. 'And nothing's going to go wrong.' She crossed her fingers superstitiously. 'You always think the worst, don't you?'

'I wonder why,' murmured Matt drily, but she heard the bitterness in his voice.

'In any case, there's a maternity unit in Padsworth—'

'A unit.' The way Matt said the words told her what he thought of that.

'And there's a large teaching hospital in the next town,' she continued staunchly.

'Which is what? Fifteen miles away? Twenty? On roads that are hardly freeways?' Matt stifled a curse. 'What if there's a late snowfall? Those narrow roads get blocked, you know that. Think what you're committing yourself to, Joanna. Much as I like your mother, she's no Florence Nightingale.'

'So what are you suggesting? That I stay in London where I can be sure of reaching a hospital that you'd consider satisfactory if there was an emergency?'

'No.'

Matt got up from the chair and pushed his hands into the pockets of his leather jacket. It put her eyes on a level with his lower body and she bent her head, trying not to think about the hard muscles that stretched his tight jeans. Or imagine how he'd looked when he was naked. She dragged her eyes away. She needed to get a grip on her emotions, not focus on what she remembered of his lean powerful body.

Matt, apparently unaware of her distraction, spoke tersely. 'I'm suggesting you come back to Cable Cay with me.' He rocked back on the heels of his boots and continued, 'There's a small house in the grounds at Long Point. A couple of bedrooms, one and a half baths. You would be perfectly comfortable there with your own staff.'

'You can't be serious!'

'Oh, I am.' Matt had never been more serious in his life. 'There's no large hospital on the island, I give you that. But I can put the helicopter I use on standby for an emergency. And there are at least three major hospitals in Nassau, half an hour away, catering to everything from insect bites to heart surgery.'

Joanna shook her head. 'But I don't want to go to the Bahamas,' she protested. She got to her feet. 'I've met the doctor in Padsworth. He knows my mother very well.'

'It's not your mother he'll be dealing with.' Matt shrugged. 'Besides, I don't think it's your decision. You owe me, Joanna. I may not have been around for most of the pregnancy, but I think I deserve to be there at my son's birth, don't you?'

CHAPTER FIFTEEN

JOANNA ASSURED HERSELF she wasn't disappointed that Matt hadn't come to meet her in Nassau. She'd taken the flight directly from London to the Bahamas and been met by Matt's helicopter pilot, Jacob Mallister, instead. He'd flown her on to Cable West, the small airport that catered to Cable Cay's commercial and personal needs, where Henry Powell, Matt's steward, was waiting to greet her.

It was good to see a familiar face. She'd met the old man before on the two occasions she and Matt had holidayed at the villa. 'Hey, there, Mrs Novak,' he exclaimed, his dark features beaming as he gave her a hand to negotiate the steps down from the aircraft. 'Aren't you a sight for sore eyes?'

'A sight, certainly,' agreed Joanna drily, glad to be on solid ground again. She didn't like helicopters. They tended to dip and sway quite alarmingly, and even the short trip from New

Providence had left her feeling slightly sick. The thought of having to do that journey again, when she was in labour, filled her with a sense of alarm.

'Well, welcome to Cable Cay,' declared Henry cheerfully. 'Did you have a good journey?'

'It was fine.' Joanna didn't mention the helicopter ride. 'But I'm glad it's over.'

'I'm sure you'll feel better once you've had a good night's rest,' he said, taking charge of her cases. 'I know Mr Matt will be glad you're here safely.'

Joanna made no comment to this. She doubted Matt would care, one way or the other. He'd given her an ultimatum: let him play a part in the remaining weeks of her pregnancy—which he regarded as only fair—or face the prospect of him petitioning for custody of the child after he was born.

She didn't know whether Matt would have done such a thing, but she decided not to take the risk. And after all, surely it was no hardship to spend weeks being pampered by servants on a semitropical island in the sun.

Now, looking about her, she had to admit that she'd forgotten how picturesque the island was. The view, even this late in the evening, was so beautiful, and, in spite of everything, she had to smile.

The sunset was just gilding the palms that edged the runway, and the heat was very welcome after the rains of January back home. She was glad now that Matt had sent the helicopter. The ferry ride from Nassau would have taken the better part of two hours, and it would have been dark before she arrived.

In the distance, she could see a beach, with the ocean creaming softly on the shoreline. A cool breeze blew in from the water, and she breathed deeply as she gazed towards the horizon. The sea might look dark now, and even a little threatening, she remembered, but when the sun rose in the morning, it would be a delight in shades of pink and green and gold.

'It is good to see you again,' Henry continued, stowing her luggage in the back of a gleaming SUV. 'I think Mr Matt's been a little lonely since he moved here. But if you don't mind me saying so, you're looking a little pale, Mrs Novak. Maybe a dose of our hot Bahamian sunshine is exactly what you need, eh?'

'You could be right,' said Joanna, realising she actually was glad to be here at last. 'How are you and Teresa these days? I thought you might have retired by now.'

'Oh, no. We're not ready for retirement, Mrs Novak,' he assured her, making sure her suitcases were safely installed. He lifted her father's old laptop, which she'd brought with her. 'Will this be okay in the back?'

'Oh, yes.' Joanna nodded. 'It's just an old machine that used to belong to my father, but I've brought some work from home, and I thought it might be useful to keep in touch with my family as well.'

'Work?' Henry pulled a face.

'I run a website,' Joanna explained. 'Didn't Matt tell you, I have shares in an art gallery in London? My partner is keen for me to keep my hand in.'

'Mr Matt probably forgot,' said Henry cheerfully. 'And it's good to keep in touch with family, too. But Mr Matt's parents don't come here like they used to when the children were small.'

Joanna couldn't deny a sense of relief at these words, but she guessed that since Oliver had had his second stroke, he didn't travel as much. It hopefully meant she wouldn't have to face Matt's mother. Which could only be a plus.

The journey to the villa didn't take long. Henry spent most of it regaling her with stories of his grandchildren and asking her if she minded that she was having a boy.

'Mr Matt told me,' he added, pulling a wry face. 'He's pretty buzzed about the whole thing. I know he can't wait to meet his son.'

'Henry—'

'Oh, I know. You and Mr Matt are divorced. But it seems to me that this baby just might bring you back together.'

Joanna was tempted to say, *don't hold your breath,* but Henry was so enthusiastic, she didn't have the heart. Instead, she endeavoured to concentrate on her surroundings, unable to prevent herself from stiffening when the gates of Long Point came into view.

They had been travelling along the winding coast road, but now Henry turned the car between the gates of the Novaks' residence. 'The guesthouse is in the grounds, about a quarter of a mile from the villa,' Henry explained easily, and she remembered Matt had told her much the same.

As if to prove a point, after passing through the gates, Henry turned the car away from the main building. A twisting track led to where a neat little single-storey dwelling nestled among the trees. 'Here we are.'

Joanna had half expected that Matt would be

waiting to meet her. But the cottage appeared to be deserted, and she told herself she was grateful to have the chance to relax before meeting her host.

Someone had indeed prepared the place for her, however. The rooms smelled fresh and inviting, and a note pinned to the door—not in Matt's hand, she noticed—informed her that a seafood salad had been prepared and was waiting in the fridge.

How kind, she thought, supporting herself with both hands in the small of her back as she followed Henry across the veranda and into the house. Whatever her doubts, Matt had evidently thought of everything.

'Will I put your bags in the bedroom, Mrs Novak?' Henry was asking, after staggering up the steps with the laptop tucked precariously under his arm.

'Yes, please,' said Joanna, quickly rescuing the small computer. Laptops weren't cheap, and she'd hate for him to drop it. 'You lead the way.'

They entered the cottage via a pleasant parlour that apparently ran from the front to the back of the house. Joanna hadn't yet got her bearings, but she thought there might be a view of the ocean from the back windows. But it was getting too dark to see tonight.

A door to one side opened into a neat kitchen. There was a comprehensive supply of appliances and a small table that was presently laid for one. Then out into a narrow hall with three more doors leading to the bedrooms and the bathroom.

The bedroom Henry showed her into was surprisingly big considering the size of the rest of the cottage, with a huge colonial bed occupying a central position. The bathroom adjoining it was reassuringly modern, with a walk-in shower and a free-standing tub.

'This is great,' she said, kicking off her wedges to feel the marble floor cool beneath her bare feet. She couldn't wait to have a quick shower. She wasn't particularly hungry, but she supposed she should try a little of the salad. Then, if Matt didn't turn up, she'd fall straight into that huge bed.

'I'll leave you now, Mrs Novak,' said Henry, hovering in the bedroom doorway. 'Mr Matt asked me to tell him when you'd arrived.'

'Did he now?' Joanna wondered if that meant Matt would be arriving later tonight.

But Henry disabused her of that notion. Glancing about him, he continued, 'He also said he'd come see you in the morning. But if there's anything else you need, don't hesitate to call.'

Joanna hesitated. 'Do you have the villa's number?' Although she was fairly sure she wouldn't be using it tonight.

'The phone has a direct line to Mr Matt's office,' explained Henry. 'Just punch in number one and that will put you through. Oh, and your cook and housekeeper will be here tomorrow morning. I'm sure they'll be happy to help you, too, in any way they can.'

'Thank you.' Joanna smiled. 'Please tell Matt I do appreciate this. And thank you for meeting me, Henry.'

'My pleasure, Mrs Novak,' he assured her smilingly, and Joanna wondered if she should tell him that she didn't call herself Mrs Novak these days.

But that could wait until tomorrow, too. Right now, she was too tired to care.

Matt was sitting on the veranda, enjoying a tumbler of whisky over ice, when Henry drove up to the villa. The older man parked the vehicle behind the house and then came up onto the veranda to report to his employer.

'All present and correct,' he said, nodding his curly grey head approvingly. 'Can I do anything else for you, sir?'

'I don't think so, Henry.' Then, as the man would

have turned away, 'Does she look okay? How was her journey?'

'Mrs Novak looks fine,' said Henry enthusiastically. 'A little pale—and tired, I think—but I guess it's been a long day.'

'I guess.' Matt was thoughtful. 'Did she like the cottage?'

'Oh, yes, sir.' Henry grinned. 'I think she loved the place at first sight. She asked me to tell you so. And when Callie and Rowena take over, I think she'll be very happy there.'

'Let's hope so,' said Matt, wishing he could be as certain. He hadn't forgotten that if it hadn't been for some manipulation on his part, Joanna would be in Cornwall by now.

'I didn't help her unpack her luggage.' Henry sounded doubtful. 'But I expect she'd prefer to do that herself anyway.

'Just a couple of cases and a laptop, that's all.'

'A laptop?' Matt was intrigued.

'Yes, she told me it had belonged to her father,' Henry agreed thoughtfully. 'She says she plans to do some work while she's here.'

'Work?' Like Henry, Matt was surprised to hear this.

'Yes, sir. Seems like the lady operates a website

for some gallery she helps to run in London,' said Henry, nodding. 'Will that be all, Mr Matt?'

He was clearly waiting to go and get his supper, and Matt nodded. 'Sure thing,' he said, raising his glass, though he wasn't altogether happy about Joanna's plans to keep working for the gallery while she was here. But, at least she was here, where he could keep an eye on her.

For a while, after the man had gone, Matt remained where he was, watching the sunset. Teresa had cooked a steak for his supper, but he'd hardly eaten a thing. He hadn't relaxed, even when his pilot, Jacob, had told him they were landing. Not until Henry had arrived to say Joanna was installed at the villa had his tension subsided.

An hour later, he left the comfort of the bamboo lounger and strolled restlessly to the edge of the veranda. Hooking his hip over the wooden rail, he gazed broodingly towards the cottage. He couldn't see anything. It was too dark. But the temptation to go and check on his visitor was strong.

He'd had serious thoughts about the future since he'd returned to the Bahamas. One thing he knew for certain was that he wanted to play an active part in his child's life. However Joanna felt, he wouldn't compromise. Angus might have robbed him of his wife, but he'd be damned if he'd rob him of his son as well.

Foolishly perhaps, Matt couldn't forget that night in Miami. Joanna had given herself to him so ardently. He had to wonder, if his father hadn't been taken ill and he'd been able to follow her to London the next day, would the outcome have been the same? Or was that just wishful thinking?

He scowled and, finishing the last of his Scotch, he got up from the rail and dropped his glass onto the table. He was getting maudlin, he thought. Discovering he was going to be a father had done that to him. Nothing else.

After all, when he'd left her apartment after following her to England, he'd had no intention of seeing her again. And, despite his comparative isolation here, he'd been managing to make a satisfactory life for himself.

He wrote most mornings, and, when he got writer's block, he had the businesses in town to check on. He'd actually been thinking he might get married again one day, although it was not a priority. But his parents wanted grandchildren and he'd had to acknowledge that as his father's only son, he had some responsibilities in that regard.

Discovering Joanna was pregnant had thrown any other plans out of the window. And learning he was going to have a son had been the icing on the cake. During the long nights, as he'd waited for her to come to the island, he'd found himself wondering if he could persuade her to stay.

But hearing about her plans to keep working, he doubted she had anything similar in mind.

He scowled into the darkness, wondering a little anxiously if she'd remembered to lock her doors. People didn't always lock their doors on Cable Cay, and it was unlikely anyone would disturb her, but Matt couldn't put it out of his mind.

The sudden piercing scream that rent the peace of the evening set Matt's heart pounding. The sound had definitely come from the cottage, and, after what he'd been thinking, his blood went cold.

Without a moment's hesitation, he leapt down the steps and started along the path to the villa, all manner of horrific scenarios racing through his mind. If anyone had invaded the cottage, he'd kill them. And if they'd touched her…

But he refused to continue that thought.

CHAPTER SIXTEEN

MATT COVERED THE quarter-mile in minutes. Before he reached the cottage, he heard someone running after him and guessed that Henry, too, had heard the scream.

'That was Mrs Novak, wasn't it?' the man panted as he caught up with Matt. 'You don't think there's an intruder, do you?' Henry persisted, and Matt was glad the older man couldn't see his face.

'I hope not,' he retorted grimly, already planning what he would do if anyone had touched Joanna.

They reached the cottage and Matt bounded up the steps to bang on the door. But there was no need to announce his arrival. The door was unlocked, and, remembering his earlier fears on Joanna's behalf, he hoped it was she who hadn't turned the key.

'Joanna!' he yelled, bursting into the parlour, and heard what he thought was a responding cry coming from the other side of the house. It was from one of the bedrooms, he thought, his nerves as taut as violin strings. What was going on?

Henry was right behind him when he reached the bedroom where the sound had come from. The door was shut, which might or might not be a good thing. But then he heard Joanna call, 'Matt! Matt, is that you?' and realised that whatever had happened, she was still okay.

However, when he opened the door, the sight that met his eyes was not at all reassuring. Joanna was standing on the bed, and she was obviously terrified. Her arms were wrapped protectively around her middle, and there was a look of real terror in her eyes.

She was wearing only a man-sized tee shirt that was so thin as to be almost transparent. It barely covered her thighs, due in no small part to the size of her stomach that swelled beneath the cloth. Long legs, bare and disturbingly familiar, caused his stomach to tighten in response.

But Matt definitely didn't want to think about that right now.

When she saw him, Joanna's relief was evident. 'Oh, thank God, you've come,' she exclaimed tremulously, forgetting for a moment that she hadn't seen him since her arrival.

Then she saw Henry hovering behind him, and half turned away in embarrassment. 'Um—there's a rat; under the bed.' A sob broke from her throat. 'Can you get rid of it? Please! It—it's huge!'

'A rat?' Matt let go of the door and came towards her, dark and disturbing in a black tee and matching shorts. Immediately the room was filled with his raw masculinity, and Joanna had to grope for a breath of cool night air. 'Are you sure?'

'I'm sure,' Joanna managed shakily, and wondered if he knew she was struggling against tears. 'It was there when I came out of the bathroom. Just—just staring at me with evil little eyes.'

Matt reserved judgement on the *evil little eyes* but it was obvious something had frightened her badly.

'So where is it now?' asked Henry, coming into the room behind him. The older man seemed unconcerned about Joanna's appearance, and Matt gave him a half-impatient look.

'She says it's under the bed,' he said, going down on one knee to scan the area in question. And then he allowed a rueful smile when he saw what was huddling beneath the wooden frame.

'What is it? What is it?' Joanna was shifting from foot to foot, and Matt was half afraid she was going to lose her balance and fall. 'Can you see it?' Then, observing his expression, 'What's so funny?'

Matt shook his head, sobering, and, getting to his feet again, he turned to Henry. 'It's a hutia,' he told the other man. 'I'd say the poor thing's more frightened than she is.'

'A hutia?' Joanna had never heard of such a thing. 'Is—is that a rat?'

'It's a rodent, certainly,' agreed Matt, as Henry bent to view the culprit. 'But it's not a rat. They're usually quite harmless. People actually keep them as pets. God knows how it got in here.' He turned to Henry again. 'Who was the last person in the cottage?'

'I suppose that would be me,' said Henry unhappily. 'I came and checked the place out before I went to the airport. I might have left the doors open for a while. It was so hot, and I wanted the breeze to blow through.'

Joanna tried to calm her erratic heartbeat. What a perfect way to start her stay on the island. She'd never screamed like that before. But then, she'd never been so frightened either. Matt probably thought she was a complete idiot.

'Can—can you get rid of it?' she asked, trying to behave more calmly now that it seemed that there was no danger.

But she was embarrassed that the older man was there.

Matt looked thoughtful. 'Well, we can,' he said, in answer to her question. 'But the whole place will have to be fumigated before you can stay here.' He turned once more to Henry. 'Why don't you go and get the SUV and we'll bring Mrs Novak back to the villa?'

Joanna's lips parted. 'Your villa?'

'You can't stay here tonight,' he added, aware that his panic on her behalf had given way to a kind of resentment. What chance did he have of keeping his cool when even her scream could tear his nerves to shreds?

He scowled. It was hard to be gentle with her when seeing her like this had aroused all the carnal instincts he'd been trying so hard to deny. For pity's sake, he'd spent the latter half of the evening trying to drown the knowledge that Joanna was here and he still wanted her. Had he ever stopped wanting her? He didn't want to know.

Meanwhile, Joanna, hearing the censure in his voice, assumed his attitude towards her hadn't changed. Bringing her here had been a way to prove his dominance, and after the cottage was habitable again, she'd try and make sure she didn't need his help again.

With Henry on his way back to the villa, Joanna hesitated only a moment longer and then dropped down onto her knees. But she was aware her heart was still racing and the baby had been unusually quiet for the past half-hour. Shocked into immobility, she thought uneasily. Honestly, whatever that creature was, it had scared both of them half to death.

'Would you like me to carry you into the bathroom,' asked Matt, noticing her uncertainty, but to his relief Joanna shook her head.

'Um—I don't think that will be necessary,' she said a little breathlessly. But she needed to put some clothes on before Henry returned. 'Will—will that—what did you call it? Hutia? —will it try to escape?'

Matt regarded her critically for a moment, and then gave in. 'It's probably more frightened of you than you are of it,' he said, his tone softening. 'It's not gonna leap out at you, if that's what you're afraid of.'

Joanna nodded and wriggled until her legs were hanging over the side of the bed. Her tee shirt had hiked up to the tops of her thighs, but that couldn't be helped. It was a bit late now to be feeling embarrassed, and she was wearing panties, after all.

The cotton trousers she'd travelled in were

draped over one of the chairs nearest the door, her slip-ons on the floor beside them. It was only a little distance, she told herself firmly. If the creature hadn't been disturbed by Matt and Henry kneeling down to peer at it, why should it bother her?

Matt was standing watching her. He had his arms folded, legs apart, his narrow-fitting shorts moulding his powerful thighs. Why did he have to look so damn sexy? she wondered, sliding her bare feet to the floor. It was becoming harder and harder to remember that this was the man who had ruined the last months of her father's life.

She straightened up, and as she did so something brushed by her ankle. She managed to stifle the scream that rose in her throat, but she couldn't prevent herself from rushing headlong towards the door.

She certainly hadn't intended to touch Matt. She just wanted to get away from the bed. But when he put out his hand to stop her reckless flight, she didn't think before wrapping her arms about his waist and cuddling close to him.

Apart from anything else, her panic had robbed her of any resistance. 'What—what was that?' she choked, her face pressed to the muscled hardness of his chest. Her hands spread against his back, accidentally connecting with the wedge of flesh exposed when he'd bent down and his tee had separated from his shorts. Struggling to ignore the smooth dampness of his skin beneath her fingers, she said hurriedly, 'I felt something touch my ankle. Was it the—the hutia?'

'Probably,' said Matt stiffly, aware that it was only the swell of her pregnancy that was keeping her from feeling his instant arousal. Dammit, he had to stay away from her or God knew what he might be tempted to do. With his tone flattening, he responded, 'It's gone now, anyway. You can let me go.'

But Joanna didn't want to let him go. With her lungs filled with the sensual heat of his body, it was difficult to think coherently about anything. She fought valiantly for breath before saying, 'Where—where do you think it went?'

'I have no idea.' Matt sighed, his hands closing on her trembling shoulders. The fabric of the shirt was so thin that he could feel the dampness of her skin through the cloth, but he forced himself to ignore the intimacy of the moment. 'I imagine it's found its way out of here.'

She swallowed. 'You don't think it could have gone into the bathroom?'

'I don't think it was heading in that direction, no.' Matt stepped back. Then, belatedly, he seemed to remember her condition, his eyes lowering to her stomach, bringing another wave of heat over her body. 'You're okay, aren't you? You didn't hurt yourself?' He paused. 'Or the baby?'

'I don't think so.'

She ran an exploring hand over her bump and felt the reassuring thrust of a foot against her palm. She smiled, relieved that the baby was active again, and saw the way Matt's expression had changed to one of concern.

'You're sure?'

'I'm sure.' She hesitated. 'Would you like to feel him?'

Matt's pulse quickened in spite of himself. 'I—well, sure,' he said half unwillingly, and she took his hand and laid it against the rounded curve of her stomach.

Almost immediately, he felt a powerful little kick against his hand, and he pulled away with a grunt of protest. 'Strong, isn't he?' Joanna asked, smiling again. 'How would you like to feel that in the early hours of the morning?'

Matt shook his head. 'I can't imagine.'

But he could, actually. It was amazingly easy to anticipate lying beside Joanna and sharing the intimacies of the pregnancy. Comforting her when the baby's activities kept her awake, holding her in his arms until she and the baby went back to sleep.

Yet that was exactly the opposite of what he should be thinking, he reminded himself irritably. 'Why don't you get dressed and put a couple of things in a bag?' he added shortly, moving towards the door. 'When Henry gets back, we'll be leaving.'

'Okay.' Joanna cast a nervous glance towards the bathroom. 'You're sure it's gone?'

'I'm sure,' said Matt, his patience shredding. 'Henry probably left the door open when he left and it will have made its escape.'

Joanna's lips tightened, seeking a defence. 'I could say it's your fault for making me come here,' she retaliated, hating the fact that right now she needed him more than he needed her. 'I should have stayed in England, with my mother and Lionel.'

'Let's not start that again,' said Matt wearily, glancing about the room and noticing the pair of drawstring trousers on the chair. 'Here.' He handed them to her. 'Do you have a shirt you can wear?'

Joanna took the trousers out of his hands. 'I expect so,' she said, stopping briefly to take a silky patterned smock from the open suitcase lying on the ottoman at the foot of the bed. She walked swiftly into the bathroom. 'I won't be long.'

CHAPTER SEVENTEEN

SURPRISINGLY, AFTER ALL the upset, Joanna slept soundly. The baby kicked a couple more times, but even he didn't disturb her for long. She was exhausted after the journey. Not to mention the stress of the very real fear she'd suffered over last evening's intruder.

The bedroom Teresa had prepared for her was cool and comfortable, and she'd fallen asleep as soon as her head touched the pillow. Of course, although she wouldn't admit it, knowing that Matt was just down the hall made all the difference.

She woke fairly early the next morning. She went into the adjoining bathroom first and took a shower, and then, after finding a bottle of water on her bedside table, she took a welcome drink before opening the door onto her veranda.

As she stepped outside, the heat was the first thing she noticed. She'd wrapped one of the enormous bath towels around her, but the atmosphere soon brought a sheen of dampness to her skin. She wondered if Matt would allow her to go swimming. The idea of silky smooth water washing over her overheated body was very appealing.

She'd swim in the ocean, of course. Attractive though the pool at the villa might be, she'd insisted on her independence.

But, after considering how she'd look in the only swimsuit she'd brought with her, she decided she'd save her dip for another day.

After another drink of the slightly warm water, she went back into her room, appreciating the coolness of conditioned air. She looked about her, admiring the stripped pine floor and silk-hung walls of the bedroom. As well as the large bed, there was a cosy sitting area with two armchairs and a circular table.

And no unwelcome visitors.

A rummage through the few garments she'd brought from the cottage turned up a pair of drawstring shorts. She frowned as she looked at them. Everything had to be elasticated or drawstring these days, she thought resignedly. It seemed such a long time since she'd been able to wear anything remotely attractive—or sexy.

It had certainly been a blow to her ego when Matt had pushed her away from him the night before. For a few moments, when he'd let her wrap her arms around him, she'd actually felt he cared about her. And he'd been so sweet when he'd put his hand on her stomach to feel the baby. But then he'd seemed to come to his senses with a vengeance.

Still, it was probably all to the good, she told herself firmly. Look where one reckless night in Miami had got her.

Matt strode down the path to where his boat was moored with a feeling of frustration. He hadn't slept well after the uproar over the damn hutia, and, although he'd taken a cold shower, he couldn't get the remembrance of Joanna's warm body, pressed against his own, out of his mind.

It was the early hours before exhaustion had claimed him, and in consequence it was now after seven o'clock, much later than he usually took to the water.

Henry was back at the villa, with strict instructions to get the cottage in order so 'Mrs Novak' could return to it today.

Even so, after last night's little fiasco, Matt had to concede that the distance between the two dwellings was much too short.

He'd never forget how he'd felt when he'd heard Joanna scream. At the very least, he'd expected to find some poisonous insect in the cottage, or, failing that, an intruder, intent on God knew what.

A lizard scuttled away as he reached the jetty, and he breathed deeply of the cool salt-laden air. He forced himself to relax. The whole expanse of Cable Bay awaited him. And out on the water, where colours shifted from pale green in the shallows to deep blue on the horizon, he'd be far away from any domestic problem Joanna might create.

A breeze blew across the surface, soft and inviting, and with it came a drift of a familiar perfume. It wasn't night-scented jasmine, or oleander, or any of the many flowering shrubs that grew in such profusion all over the island. This perfume was sensual; individual. So who the hell had invaded his private beach?

Did he really have to guess?

And then he saw her.

Joanna was wading in the shallows at the edge of the beach beyond the jetty. She'd secured her hair on top of her head this morning, and several errant strands curled against her nape. She was wearing shorts and a loose-fitting shirt that looked suspiciously like one of his. And although her legs were long, judging by the depth of the water around her, he suspected the hems of her shorts were already wet.

She hadn't seen him yet, but she must have noticed the dinghy, rocking at its mooring. The bow caused a sucking sound as it nudged the wooden jetty, the mast lines chiming on the swell. Matt knew that as soon as he started releasing the cleats and it moved out into the water, she couldn't fail to hear him. He didn't want to startle her, as much for his own peace of mind as hers, but what the hell else could he do?

Go back to the villa, he thought irritably. Before she realised he was there. He'd have to give up his morning sail for once. Either that or take the chance that she might think he was following her.

He scowled, preparing to turn away, but just at that moment Joanna looked back over her shoulder and saw him. Immediately, her face flushed with becoming colour, and, abandoning whatever she'd been doing, she waded back to the shore.

She was barefoot, he noticed, as she padded back to the jetty. And although her expression was pleasant enough, she would have passed him with just a brief, 'Good morning' if Matt hadn't stepped into her path.

'You don't have to leave on my account,' he said neutrally, and Joanna's lips tilted for a moment before straightening again.

'I'm going back for breakfast,' she said, matching his casual tone. 'Teresa wasn't up when I left the villa. She's probably wondering where I am.'

'Haven't you had anything to drink?' Matt sounded scandalised. 'Don't you know you should never venture out in this heat without bringing a bottle of water with you?'

'Actually I drank a bottle of water before I left the villa,' she told him stiffly. 'I'm not a complete fool. I know what dehydration is.'

Matt was regarding her doubtfully even so, and she had to admit her mouth was dry. She smoothed the shirt she was wearing over her bump with a certain amount of embarrassment. She'd found this shirt in one of the drawers in her room, and guessed it belonged to Matt. She hadn't expected him to see her wearing it, but, now he had, she doubted he'd wear it again.

He looked so cool and relaxed in narrow-fitting shorts and a purple polo, his muscled forearms deeply tanned from the sun. His hair had been tousled by the breeze, and tumbled over his forehead, the evidence of the shower he'd taken glistening on the rich dark strands.

'Anyway,' she continued, 'as you can see, I borrowed your shirt. I hope you don't mind.'

'And if I do, are you going to take it off?' His words were provocative and he instantly regretted them. 'Forget it,' he said. 'You can wear anything of mine you like.'

Which was also provocative, but his reaction to her unspoiled beauty was uncontrollable. What on earth had possessed him to bring her here?

'Well...' Joanna licked her lips now. 'I'll see it's laundered and returned to you.'

He was sure she would. He was equally sure he'd never be able to wear the shirt again without seeing her in it. Was she wearing a bra? He didn't think so. He could see the hard nipples pressed against the cloth.

Dear God!

'Well, I'm sorry if you were worried about me,' she added politely. 'Now if you'll excuse me...'

Matt's lips tightened. 'Worried about you?' he exclaimed, realising suddenly that, as he'd suspected earlier, she had got entirely the wrong impression. 'I wasn't looking for you, if that's what you think.' He nodded towards the dinghy. 'I intended to take my boat out, that was all.'

'Oh.'

Matt expelled a harsh breath. 'In any case, you should have told someone where you were going.'

'Why?' Joanna's violet eyes widened. 'Are you saying I can't do anything here without you knowing about it?'

Matt blinked. 'Forgive me, but you seemed glad to see me last night,' he retorted, irritation causing his temper to spike. 'Or would you have preferred to have got rid of the creature yourself?'

Joanna lifted her arms, the shirt slipping sensuously off one shoulder. 'That's different,' she said defensively, but it was difficult for Matt to focus on her words.

As she'd lifted her arms, Matt had been treated to a glimpse of the dusky hollow visible below the lapels. He didn't want to notice, but once again he couldn't help himself. And another part of his body noticed, too.

He was pathetic, he told himself, as his shaft stirred instinctively at the glimpse of her breasts. It wasn't as if he hadn't seen them before. The way they'd looked that night in Miami was all too easy to remember.

Rocking back on the heels of his loafers, he managed a cynical smile. 'Do I take it you'll cope with any emergency from now on?'

Joanna wrapped her arms across her midriff and turned to stare out over the water. 'Can we not do this?' she asked, suddenly sounding weary. 'I just don't like being checked up on, that's all. I had enough of that when—when—'

'When Daddy was alive?' suggested Matt drily.

'No,' declared Joanna at once, although her father had wanted to know where she was every minute they'd been together. 'I don't know what I was going to say. It's not important. Like you said, it is very hot, and I'm going back to the villa right now.'

Matt hesitated. 'Do you want me to come with you?'

Joanna cast a brief glance in his direction, her eyes wary. 'I can manage on my own,' she said stiffly. 'Please, take your boat out. If indeed that was what you originally intended.'

She waited half apprehensively for his response, but if Matt was angry at her defiance, he didn't reply.

A couple of weeks later, Joanna had got used to living on Cable Cay.

The cottage had become her home and she was reasonably happy there. Henry—not Matt—had taken her into town a few days after her arrival to see a Dr Rodrigues, and he'd pronounced that all was well. Indeed, he'd complimented her on her good health, saying that if all pregnancies were like hers, he'd be out of a job.

Despite a certain tension between them, Matt had taken to calling round to see her every couple of days. He'd said it was to assure himself that she had everything she needed, but she couldn't deny she looked forward to his visits.

In spite of their differences, they had been married for over four years before they'd split up and they knew one another well. Certain words, certain locations, inspired a similar reaction, and, although Matt would never have believed it, they spent a lot of time reminiscing about things that had made them both laugh.

The days when she didn't see him became dull days indeed.

Although she kept in touch with David Bellamy and her mother via email—and worked on the website when David sent her details of some new exhibition he was putting on—what she enjoyed most was sitting on the veranda, sharing coffee and some of Rowena's delicious muffins with Matt. Occasionally, he discussed his work, usually some article or other he was researching, and she offered him ideas of other articles he could write.

She doubted he found her appearance particularly appealing. She hated looking in mirrors these days, especially after she'd had a bath. It was so unfair, she thought gloomily, when it was impossible to avoid her naked body. Men got women pregnant, without any of the consequences, and then stood back and let nature take its course.

To her relief, there'd been no sign of her erstwhile mother-in-law. Matt didn't mention his parents at all, except when she asked about his father. She had thought that Adrienne might arrive to check up on her, but she supposed it was just possible that Matt hadn't told his mother she was here. Though that was hardly believable, in the circumstances. There was always the chance that they might arrive here unannounced.

Matt had also put a car at her disposal and she'd actually taken a couple of trips into the small town of Cable Cay on her own. The roads were fairly good, and she'd enjoyed the feeling of independence it had given her. Although she had to admit, she'd usually chosen a morning when Matt was unlikely to appear.

Although the town wasn't very big, it was amazingly well equipped, catering to visitors and locals alike. There were small supermarkets and clothes shops, as well as the inevitable duty-free liquor stores. Joanna had spent a whole morning wandering around the open-air market.

An agency advertising deep-sea fishing and water sports had briefly attracted her attention on her second visit, mostly because the name over the door had read M.O. Novak. Matt had told her about the companies he had invested in, and she couldn't deny a certain feeling of pride that he'd confided in her.

It was a far cry from the Novak Corporation, which, as Matt had told her, Sophie was running now. He seemed to have settled down to life in the Bahamas, and she had to admit it was a good life in many ways.

Joanna had also made friends with the two women Matt had employed to cook and clean for her. The older of the two, Rowena, lived in Cable Cay. The younger, Callie, was Henry and Teresa's granddaughter, and she lived in the annexe that adjoined the villa with them.

Joanna hadn't ventured down to the beach again in the early morning. Now that she knew Matt took his boat out most days, she hadn't wanted to intrude again. Instead, she'd taken to having a stroll along the sands in the early evening. It was cooler then, and she didn't mind being on her own.

She occasionally heard the SUV leave the villa after breakfast. Callie had told her that her grandfather did most of the shopping and that it was probably him going into town. Matt had converted one of the bedrooms at the villa into his office and that was where he spent much of the day, if he had articles to write; articles Joanna found herself looking for regularly in the local gazette.

One morning, about three weeks after she'd moved into the cottage, Joanna heard the SUV leave soon after eight o'clock. Which was earlier than usual. If Henry was going shopping, he usually left between nine and ten. Was it possible it was Matt who'd gone into town?

There was no way of finding out without going down to the jetty. If the dinghy wasn't there, she'd know he was still around. He rarely took his boat out for longer than a couple of hours; not long enough for what she had in mind.

It was already hot, but Joanna was getting used to the climate. She'd acquired a golden tan and she was sure her hair was lighter now than when she'd arrived. As she spent most of her days outside, soaking up the sunshine, it wasn't surprising. She rarely stayed indoors, even when she was doing her job.

Afternoons were when she used her father's laptop. Sitting on the veranda, she sometimes marvelled at how easily she'd settled in. There were usually messages from David and her mother, asking how she was feeling. But these days she seldom wished that she were back in England.

Now, hearing the car depart, she decided to take the chance that it was Matt who had gone into town. The fact was, she'd wanted to go swimming ever since she'd arrived on the island, but she hadn't wanted Matt to see her in her swimsuit. The island attracted slim blondes and brunettes in skimpy bikinis, and Joanna was aware that the comparison couldn't have been more acute.

But the beach area was private and if Matt was away, she'd feel confident on her own. Well, she could cope with a few fish and maybe a pelican or two. The large birds tended to comb the beach in search of sand crabs or flotsam, but they were harmless enough and kept other predators at bay.

Joanna put on her swimsuit before she left the cottage.

It was navy blue with white piping around the hem of the briefs. It had a tank top to accommodate her swollen belly, and she added a multi-coloured wrap she'd bought when she was in Cable Cay. A canvas bag held water—she'd taken Matt's advice and never left the cottage without it—sunglasses and a tube of sunscreen. She carried a towel over her shoulder, and managed to slip away without either of the other women seeing her.

The dinghy was still at its mooring, so she dropped the bag and her wrap on the beach near the roots of a palm tree and laid her towel on top. Then, not wasting any time, she walked down the sandy slope and into the water. It wasn't warm, but it wasn't cold either, and she revelled in the feeling of freedom it gave her.

It was so good to wade out of her depth and feel the weight lifted from her. For the first time in months, she didn't feel dragged down by the tiny human being growing inside. Striking out with a lazy breaststroke, she swam a little distance away from the shore. Then rolled onto her back and let the water carry her on.

It was heavenly. Even the sun didn't feel so hot out here. Obviously, this was why Matt took his boat out early in the morning. To enjoy a cooler temperature before the heat set in.

Her eyes closed and she drifted on the tide, feeling totally at peace with herself and the world. How long was it since she'd been in the sea? Not since last year at Padsworth. She'd gone to spend a few days with her parents in early summer. And then, on her return, David had offered her the chance to become a partner in the gallery. He had also suggested that unless she and Matt were planning on getting back together, she should seriously think about getting a divorce.

Reminded of the divorce and of where she was

now, Joanna opened her eyes. Turning over, she got her bearings, and then gave a little gasp of dismay. While she'd been daydreaming, the tide had carried her quite some distance from the shore. It had evidently been going out when she'd entered the water, and now she was going to have to swim the better part of half a mile back to the beach.

Panic flared in the pit of her stomach. She had never been a particularly strong swimmer. When she was a kid, a couple of lengths of the local swimming baths had been more than enough for her.

Treading water, she took a deep breath, calculating the distance in her mind. She could do this, she told herself. She would have to. She'd told no one where she was going, and if Matt was away, there was no one else to come to her rescue...

Matt was still asleep when he heard someone hammering on his bedroom door.

He'd had a pretty rotten night. He seldom slept well these days, and he'd sometimes wondered if it would have been easier to relax if he'd known Joanna was just down the hall.

It didn't help that he was expecting visitors tomorrow. He hadn't told Joanna because he'd known how she would react to the news. In consequence, he'd spent half the night downing a fifth of Jack Daniels, and the other half fighting nightmares, that had left him wide awake and sweating like a pig.

It was an effort to open his eyes when the hammering on his door started. He must have fallen asleep in the early hours and now he was heavy-eyed and not in the best of tempers either.

'What the hell is going on?' he demanded, springing out of bed.

Teresa gazed at him unhappily. 'I'm sorry to disturb you, Mr Matt, but Mrs Novak has disappeared. When Callie brought her breakfast, she wasn't in her room, and, although we've searched the grounds, we don't know where she's gone.'

CHAPTER EIGHTEEN

JOANNA SAW MATT emerge from the palms beside the jetty.

He'd seen her, of course he had, she thought,
her initial relief giving way to resignation. He
was going to think she was the world's biggest
idiot. She should have told someone where she
was going and stayed in the shallows. That would
have been the sensible thing to do.

Matt's voice echoed over the water. 'Do you
need any help?'

Joanna sighed. She wanted to say, *I can manage,*
but she knew that wasn't precisely true. Nevertheless, she shook her head and started swimming
back towards the shore. It was only a little distance,
she told herself. And, after all, what could Matt do?

She found out a few tiring minutes later when
she was still a few yards out from the beach.
She'd paused for a moment, trying to regulate
her breathing, when she saw Matt tear off his shirt
and plunge into the water.

His strong crawl brought him swiftly within range of her exhausted strokes, and she knew when he reached her there were tears in her eyes. 'Thank you,' she said, when he wrapped an arm around her waist. 'I know I'm stupid.' Then, defensively, 'But I would have made it on my own.'

Matt made no comment about how unlikely that was or how stupid she'd been and she was grateful. Instead, he slicked back his hair with his free hand, and she found herself thinking rather foolishly how much she liked looking at him, even when her limbs were trembling with exhaustion and she badly wanted to cry.

His dark features seemed to have acquired a dangerous edge since he'd learned about the baby, and right now, although he hadn't said anything yet, she knew he wasn't pleased with her.

Which was a shame, because they'd been getting on so well. But the guarded gleam in his eyes warned of possible retribution to come.

Would she really have made it on her own if he hadn't come to her assistance? That was something she didn't want to think about right now. The fact was, she owed him, and she doubted he'd let her forget it.

It took an amazingly short space of time before Joanna felt shifting sand beneath her feet. Her toes touched the ground only briefly as Matt gained his feet. Then, turning, he swung her up into his arms. He carried her out of the water and up the beach, only halting when he'd reached the place where she'd left her belongings.

Joanna was suddenly inordinately breathless. But this time it wasn't because of her swim. It was the muscled strength of the arm beneath her thighs; the bronzed hardness of his chest brushing sensuously against her breasts. The awareness of her own vulnerability in the face of someone so aggressively male.

It made her realise her tank top had ridden up exposing her midriff. Not the most alluring sight, she thought unhappily, but she couldn't do anything about it now. All she knew was that Matt was staring down at her, the dark penetration of his heavy-lidded eyes making her wonder if he'd just tumbled out of bed.

'What possessed you to swim so far out on your own?' he demanded. 'You always said you weren't a strong swimmer.'

'I'm not,' she said unhappily. 'Were you in town? Did Henry get in touch with you and tell you what I was doing?'

'There wouldn't have been much point in telling me if I'd been in town, would there?' Matt asked reasonably. 'Besides, it's Henry who's in town. It was Teresa who warned me what was going on. Callie came rushing over to the villa saying you'd disappeared.'

Joanna felt dreadful. 'I'm sorry,' she said, aware that her voice was still shaky. 'You can put me down now.'

But, God help her, being this close to him was both a pleasure and a torment. She couldn't deny it any longer. Whatever he'd done, she still wanted to be with him. Surely it wasn't just her chaotic hormones causing her to lose all resistance to this man. Regardless of their past mistakes, was she willing to begin again?

Was he?

When he lowered her feet to the sand, and her rounded belly slid the length of his muscular frame, desire got the better of her. Without giving it a second thought, she wound her arms around his neck, and brought her parted lips to his.

Matt stiffened instinctively. He might have suspected that, despite her denials, Joanna had never been indifferent to him. But in spite of the way she'd behaved since she'd been here, he'd assumed she was still planning on going back to England after the baby was born.

And he'd thought he'd accepted it, until today.

Teresa had only had to knock on his door and tell him that Joanna had disappeared, for him to tumble out of bed and race madly to find her.

But what did she really want from him? Temporary consolation? And why in God's name did he care? He had to remember it was she who'd wanted the divorce in the first place. Would things have been different if she'd succeeded in contacting him? If Laura Reichert hadn't answered the phone when she rang?

He'd moved on, he reminded himself. Or he'd thought he had. He'd made a decent life for himself here. He had to remember that.

Joanna was staring at him now with anxious eyes. With her arms wrapped around his neck, her fingers tangled in the damp thickness of his hair, this was where she wanted to be. But Matt had dragged his mouth away from hers and his hands had moved to her shoulders, closing almost cruelly over the tender sunburned flesh.

'What the hell do you think you're doing?' he demanded, and the emotion in his voice was raw and painful to his ears. 'If this is your way of thanking me for saving you, I don't need it.'

He spoke almost brutally and Joanna's lips parted in dismay. 'It wasn't meant to be a way of thanking you,' she said tremulously. 'What do you think I am?'

'I don't know, do I?' retorted Matt, knowing he was being deliberately cruel. But he had to get away from her. It would be far too easy to succumb again.

His life felt as if it had been put on hold ever since he'd found out about the pregnancy. He'd told her he was determined to play a part in his son's life, and he was. But in all honesty, knowing he still cared about her, getting her to spend the last couple of months of her pregnancy on Cable Cay had definitely not been the most sensible thing to do.

He had to keep his head, he told himself. Joanna was feeling lonely, that was all, and maybe a little hungry for affection, too. Well, he knew that feeling. Yet surely, he had more sense than to think that reckless sex with her would fill the hollow shell he'd become?

Nevertheless, there was something oddly erotic about a woman who was carrying his child. He was responsible for the life that was growing inside her. It was his seed that had changed her perfect life.

'Okay, so if this isn't gratitude, what is it?' he asked harshly.

Joanna's eyes filled once again with tears. And despite the heat of the sun on her shoulders, inside she suddenly felt as cold as ice. She pulled her hands from his shoulders and took a step back from him. 'I'm sorry. Obviously, I've made another mistake.'

Joanna caught her breath, wrapping her arms about herself in an effort to restore some warmth to her body. She should never have started this, she realised unsteadily, but she'd been fool enough to think he must still care about her.

She would have brushed past him then. Her towel and the wrap she'd worn before her swim were only a few feet away, and she'd feel better with something to warm her. Something to hide, not just her bump, but her humiliation.

Matt caught her arm as she swung past him and brought her round to face him. 'So what do you want now?' he demanded, and she trembled in the grip of emotions too long denied.

'I—I want you, Matt,' she said, her voice low and defensive, and, with a muffled oath, Matt's resistance collapsed.

With a groan of defeat, he reached for her, pulling her into his arms and covering her trembling lips with his. It was what he'd wanted to do, God knew, since he'd gathered her up out of the water.

He'd been kidding himself that he could control the needs she aroused in him.

Joanna didn't know how her legs continued to support her. The savage pressure of his mouth on hers had her clutching the waistband of his shorts with both hands. She clung to him helplessly, desperate to redeem herself. Anything to avoid subsiding like a sack of potatoes at his feet.

A reluctant shiver of anticipation made its way down her spine as he continued to kiss her. Her heart beat with a slow, heavy resonance, almost deafening to her ears. The beat thudded against his chest so that she was sure he must be able to feel it. And her skin, which moments before had felt damp and chilled, was now turning her blood to fire.

Matt lifted his head, his eyes meeting hers, an unwilling hunger in their depths. Then he bent his head again and took one burgeoning nipple into his mouth. His tongue circled the tender tip, so that it hardened instinctively. The thin fabric of her tank top was no barrier to his searching mouth.

With a low moan, she slipped the straps off her shoulders, exposing her breasts to his possessive gaze. She watched him as he ran his knuckles back and forth across the sensitive peaks, enjoying his quickening breathing, and saw the words of protest die unspoken on his lips.

'So beautiful,' he whispered.

She swallowed convulsively before saying weakly, 'Are you sure this is what you want?'

'I thought it was what you wanted,' he responded roughly, and Joanna sucked in a breath.

'You know it is,' she said, unable to deny it, and with an oath of submission Matt picked her up and carried her into the shade of the trees.

Her towel made a makeshift couch and he laid her on it.

'God, should I be doing this?' he muttered. 'I don't know anything about these things. Will I hurt you?'

'Don't worry,' she breathed, gazing eagerly up at him. 'Believe me, I'm not made of glass.'

Without another word, he dropped his own shorts onto the sand and then stripped the panties of her swimsuit from her. When he was lying naked between her legs, she pulled his face down to hers to trace his lips with her tongue. Time spiralled; she was hardly aware of where she was any more. All she knew for certain was that this was where she'd longed to be.

His kisses grew harder, more passionate, until she was practically mindless with delight. Her hands slid down his chest to take his erection between her palms, her fingers threading through the nest of rough dark hair at his groin. She caressed him and whispered, 'You used to like me to do this,' and Matt's answering groan was muffled against her throat.

Somehow, he dragged her hands away and parted her thighs with an unsteady hand. 'God, Jo,' he said. 'You make me crazy. This is crazy, but I don't want it to end.'

Her breath hitched with excitement as he bent towards her and then he was burying his face in the moist curls at the junction of her legs. He had barely to touch her, and she climaxed. Then his tongue stroked the tiny nub of her sex and she lost control again.

His fingers parted her, and she arched beneath him. She craved the feel of his hands, the hungry pressure of his mouth. 'Please,' she said, clutching his hair and dragging his lips up to hers. 'I can't wait any longer. I want you; I want you inside me. Now.'

Her voice was thick with emotion, and with a muffled oath he gave in to her demands. 'Do you think I don't want to be inside you?' he asked, licking his lips, tasting her essence. 'I've thought of little else since you came here.'

Joanna found that incredibly hard to believe. But Matt was leaning over her now, trying not to hurt her or the baby, and she was so wet and ready for him, he couldn't hold back. With a feeling of total indulgence, he let his erection tentatively ease inside her. And as her muscles stretched to accommodate him, he pushed himself deeply into her slick sheath.

God, it was good. So good. Familiar, yet unfamiliar, and all the better for the months they'd been apart. The velvety feel of her muscles closing around him was incredible. She was tight, so tight, he was sure no other man had touched her. She'd been a virgin the first time he'd made love to her, and he felt as if he were making love to a virgin again.

Joanna wound her arms around him, the scent of her arousal enfolding him in a haze of passion. His mouth sought hers again, delighting in the sensuous battle of their tongues. Her breath was sweet, her words of pleasure erotic. They were like heaven to his ears, and he lost himself in sensual need.

He cupped the rounded curves of her bottom, lifting her to accommodate his throbbing shaft. Pressing forward, he filled her again and again, pleasure uncoiling inside him. She was so tight, so wet, and he wanted to share it with her; to share the satisfying sense of atonement that nothing else could replace.

His release was uncontrollable. As soon as he felt her body clenching around his shaft, he was forced to let go. His last coherent thought was the need to roll onto his side so he didn't crush her. Before the irresistible pull of exhaustion dragged his tired eyelids closed.

CHAPTER NINETEEN

MATT REALISED HE must have slept for a few minutes because when he opened his eyes, Joanna was on her feet, her swimsuit restored, bending over him.

She had evidently been shaking him, and when his eyes opened, she murmured softly, 'Someone's calling you. You'd better get dressed.'

Matt was inclined to say he didn't much care, but it was obvious Joanna didn't want the embarrassment of one of his staff finding him in the nude.

'Who is it?' he asked, pushing himself up into a sitting position and reaching for his shorts. 'Henry?'

'No, I think it's Teresa,' replied Joanna in a low voice. 'She's probably wondering where you've gone.'

He pulled on his shorts and picked up his discarded polo shirt, which Joanna must have collected from further down the beach. The fabric clung to his still damp body, and Joanna thought it was as sexy in its way as his bare skin.

Her tongue circling her upper lip, she said nervously, 'Are you all right?'

'I guess so. Are you?'

It was a simple question, but Joanna didn't have an answer. Yes, she was okay; yes, she'd loved making love with him; but God knew where they went from here.

'I think so,' she said finally, reaching for her wrap and draping it about her shoulders. 'I suppose I should be getting back to the cottage.'

Matt shrugged, but his face had tightened, and she couldn't help feeling anxious. Was he already regretting what they'd done? Whatever she was feeling, it wasn't regret, she acknowledged honestly. But she had never felt more apprehensive in her life.

Before Matt could say anything more, however, Teresa appeared on the jetty. Her dark face was concerned, but when she saw Joanna and Matt together, her lips parted in a wide smile.

'Oh, there you are, Mrs Novak,' she exclaimed with evident relief. 'We were so worried about you, weren't we, Mr Matt? My granddaughter didn't know where you'd gone.'

'I'm sorry—' began Joanna, but before she could continue, Matt intervened.

'Mrs Novak decided to take a swim,' he said, making no mention of his part in bringing her back to shore. 'Perhaps you'd apologise to Callie. I'm sure my—Joanna—regrets not informing you what she was planning to do.'

Matt wasn't looking at her and she smiled at the housekeeper instead. 'That's right,' she said. 'It was a little foolish.' It was easier to admit her mistake. 'But it was such a lovely morning and I haven't had a swim since I arrived.'

Teresa frowned. 'You could always use the pool,' she said, looking at Matt, but he didn't say anything. 'Oh, well,' she continued, purposely cheerful. 'No harm done.'

Her eyes lingered for a moment on Joanna's belly, and Joanna assured herself that Teresa couldn't possibly know what had been going on. She was sure her hair was mussed and there was probably sand coating her thighs. But hopefully the housekeeper would assume she'd been sitting on the beach after her swim and not indulging in hot, sweaty sex.

Now, Teresa glanced back towards the villa, and said, 'Anyway, I'd better get back to my kitchen.

With visitors coming this afternoon—' She pulled a wry face. 'There's still quite a lot to do.'

Offering another polite smile, she hurried away, and Joanna bent to pick up her towel. Shaking it free of sand, she said curiously, 'Visitors? I didn't know you were expecting company.'

Matt shrugged. 'I doubt if you'll be pleased to hear who it is.'

Joanna waited for him to go on, but he didn't. She thought she could guess the identity of his visitors after what he'd just said, but it was hard not to feel excluded from his life.

Gathering her belongings, she avoided his eyes as she said, 'Well, give your parents my best, won't you? Particularly your father. Tell him he's welcome to come to the cottage any time.'

'Okay.' Matt blew out a breath. 'I guess I'll see you tomorrow.'

'Will you have time for me, now that you've got visitors?' Joanna asked, aware that she sounded resentful. 'I doubt if your mother will want to see me again.'

Matt heaved a sigh. 'My mother coming here has nothing to do with us. What happened, happened, Jo. You know it and I know it. You wanted me, and you're pretty good at getting your own way.'

Joanna felt sick. 'Well, at least I know where I

stand,' she said stiffly, bundling the towel about her. 'I know I don't look very appealing at the moment, but I could do without you making me feel like a desperate housewife!'

That hadn't been his intention, and now Matt felt guilty. 'It wasn't a criticism,' he muttered gruffly. 'But for pity's sake, Jo, you need to decide what it is you want from me.'

With an effort, Joanna managed to stem the tears that burned behind her eyes. 'Go and get ready for your guests. I'm sure they'll be better company than I am.'

'I doubt it.' Matt's tone was gentler now. 'My mother thought the trip would give my father something to think about besides his health.'

'Oh—' Joanna pressed a hand to her throat. 'But they do know I'm staying here?'

'They know,' agreed Matt, picking up her wrap and removing the towel to drape the silk shawl over her shoulders. He was tempted to bend his head and kiss the soft curve of her nape, but he restrained himself. His eyes darkened with some concern. 'You are okay? I mean with what just happened. I didn't hurt you?'

'No, you didn't hurt me,' she replied, although the ache in her heart told a different tale, but she couldn't let him see how she really felt.

Matt heaved a breath and glanced back towards the villa. He wasn't proud of what he'd done, particularly after he'd promised himself this wouldn't happen again. Yet here he was, having just enjoyed the most delightful sex of his life and he was looking for reasons to blame her for his weakness.

Dammit, why did Joanna have to be so sexy? Even in her present condition, he'd never wanted any other woman. Was that why his attraction to her was so addictive? Because his feelings towards her couldn't be replaced? He had the feeling he wouldn't like the answer. It had always been that way with her.

'So,' he said, trying to defuse the situation. 'So long as you're okay, I'd better be getting back.' He glanced down at his legs, which, like hers, were coated with sand. 'I need a shower and I'm sure you do, too.' He paused. 'If Henry's home, I'll get him to drive you back to the cottage. It will save you walking so far in this heat.'

'I'd prefer to walk,' declared Joanna at once, even though her legs still felt like jelly. Her lips twisted. 'Give your mother my regards, won't you? I'm sure she'll appreciate the irony.'

'Jo!'

But she didn't stop, and Matt decided it wouldn't

be wise to go after her. He needed time—hell, they both needed time—to come to terms with what came next.

When she got back to the cottage, the first thing Joanna did was run herself a bath.

Her legs were covered in sand, yes, and she didn't like the gritty feeling on her skin. But despite what she'd told Matt, her back was aching, and she felt a warm bath might ease the stiffness in her bones.

Callie knocked on the door as Joanna was drying herself. 'Would you like an iced tea, Mrs Novak?' she asked, with a certain amount of diffidence. She was evidently feeling guilty for causing such a panic over Joanna's disappearance.

Joanna sighed, wrapping the huge bath towel around her and opening the door. 'That sounds good,' she said, earning a relieved smile from the young woman waiting outside. 'Sorry if I worried you earlier. I'll be out in about ten minutes.'

Deciding it was too warm, even for shorts, Joanna slipped a loose cotton caftan over her head. The ankle-length dress, patterned in shades of green and apricot, was cool and comfortable. She'd bought it at a boutique on one of her trips to town. Typical tourist wear.

She'd washed her hair, too, and she left it loose about her shoulders. She didn't expect to see anyone, other than the two women who worked at the cottage. She was sure Matt would have his hands full if his parents were coming to stay.

It was a day for relaxing, she decided, as though most days didn't fall into that category anyway. Maybe it would be a good day to check up on what was happening in the rest of the world.

With that purpose in mind, she carried the worn leather case containing her father's old laptop out onto the veranda, where Callie had left her a tray of iced tea and a dish of newly baked muffins. She was going to be horribly fat when this was over, she thought ruefully, taking one of the muffins and biting into the rich fruity filling. She doubted David would appreciate his new partner looking like a blimp.

Thinking of David reminded her that after the baby was born, she'd be going back to London. It was no longer an appealing prospect, but after today she was only fooling herself if she thought that Matt was going to change his mind about her. She could feel the baby moving energetically inside her. A particularly sharp kick, just below her ribcage, had her wincing at the unexpected blow.

Was Matt's son exacting the revenge his father was denied?

Finishing her muffin, Joanna drank some of the iced tea and then set her glass aside. Pulling the laptop towards her, she unzipped the case and pulled out the old computer. She didn't know why she bothered putting it in its case really. It was hardly in pristine condition.

The last time she'd used it, she'd scanned some of her father's old emails. She'd hoped she might find something about the accident and what his re-action had been. But Angus had evidently kept his business correspondence in an encrypted folder, and she didn't have the password, or there was nothing about the case to find.

The only anomaly, which she'd just read the evening before, was an email from a betting web-site. It was a demand for money, informing her father that he was several hundred pounds in the red. Obviously, whoever had sent the email didn't know Angus had died, and, knowing what her fa-ther had always thought about gambling, she ig-nored it. She had intended to mention it to Matt the next time she saw him. But after this morn-ing's episode, that might be some distance in the future.

She pulled the computer out of its case, as usual,

but this time a worn scrap of paper fell to the floor. Bending to pick it up, she saw it was a letter. And judging by its shabby appearance, it was probably older than the computer itself.

Frowning, she unfolded the page, wondering how long it had been there. It must have been lodged in one of the compartments, and because there were so many tears in the paper it was written on, it hadn't dropped out straight away. Back in London, she used the computer at the gallery to do her work, and it was only since she'd been here that it had been of any use.

The letter she'd rescued was dated June 1980, and Joanna whistled through her teeth. Goodness—that was almost forty years ago. Why on earth would her father keep a letter that long? Surely it must have been written while he was still at university?

Was the letter from her mother? It started *Darling Angus* and that was a very intimate form of address. Turning the page, Joanna looked for her mother's signature. But instead it read *Much love, Adrienne.*

Adrienne!

The address was Girton College, Cambridge. *Girton!* Her mother had attended one of the London universities. Had her father been involved with this woman before he and Glenys had got together? Had her mother known about this other woman in her father's life?

Joanna frowned, turning back to the front of the letter and reading the address again. Whoever had written it had been a student at Girton College. Her father had been at Trinity College, Cambridge, but that was all she knew.

She felt a little guilty, reading a letter that had so obviously been addressed to her father. But, as with the emails, it couldn't hurt him now. Besides, she was only human. And she was curious.

Reading on, she frowned in concentration.

Darling Angus,
It isn't easy for me to write this letter, my dear, but I'm afraid I can't see you again. We've had some wonderful times together, and I'm going to miss you, terribly. But you must have realised, as I did, that it couldn't go on for ever, I'm going back to the States to marry Oliver—

Joanna broke off, her jaw dropping. *Oliver!* Was this letter from Adrienne Novak? she wondered incredulously. Although of course, Adrienne's surname hadn't been Novak in those days.

She read on.

It will make all the difference to my family. He's promised to help Daddy financially, and you know I could never live on a shoestring, my dear. I'm returning to New York at the end of the week. But before I left I wanted to wish you every happiness for the future. I'm sure you and Glenys—

Joanna's jaw dropped. She couldn't help it. It was one thing to speculate if her father had had an affair and quite another to have it confirmed.

—will get married as you originally intended. I don't think either of us took our relationship seriously. I know I didn't. We're two different people, Angus. It's been fun while it lasted, but like all good things it must sadly come to an end.
Much love...

Joanna was stunned. The tone of the letter really irritated her. She wondered if her father and mother had been engaged at the time. If they had, this was such a betrayal. She doubted her mother knew anything about it, and it certainly showed

Angus's outrage at his wife's departure for the hypocrisy it had been.

She wondered why her father had kept the letter for so many years. Had he had some intention of using it for his own ends? Why else would he have kept it, unless he'd had some ulterior motive for doing so? Which undoubtedly cast a shadow over other things he'd done.

Was that why Adrienne had always hated her? Had she been afraid that Angus might tell Oliver about their affair? It must have been a bitter irony that her son should have fallen in love with Angus's daughter. No wonder she'd tried her best to keep them apart.

Did it also explain why her father had been so willing to merge his company with NovCo? And why, initially, he hadn't opposed her marriage to Matt? The accident had brought things to a head, of course, and he'd involved her in it. But could the accusations Angus had made against Matt and his father now be seen in a different light?

CHAPTER TWENTY

JOANNA WAS IN the kitchen, talking to Rowena, when Callie came to tell her she had a visitor. 'It's Mr Novak,' she said in a hushed voice. 'My grandfather brought him over.'

Mr Novak? For a moment Joanna couldn't think what she meant. And then she realised: it must be Matt's father. Dared she hope his wife hadn't come with him?

Although the Novaks had arrived a couple of days ago, Joanna hadn't seen them. She'd heard from Callie that Mr Matt's father spent most of his days in a wheelchair, but she'd also said he was cheerful enough, and obviously pleased to be here.

With a hasty examination of her appearance, Joanna followed the girl into the parlour. But both Oliver Novak and Henry Powell were waiting for her on the veranda; Oliver in his electric wheelchair and Henry standing proudly beside him.

'Here she is,' said Oliver at once, only the faint slur in his speech revealing the lingering effects of his stroke. 'It's a pleasure to see you again, Jo. Come and give an old man a kiss.'

Joanna smiled and went to hug Matt's father warmly. 'It's great to see you, too,' she said, regarding him with real affection. 'It must be nearly two years since we last met.'

'At least,' agreed Oliver, glancing up at the man at his side. Then he said, 'You go and visit with your granddaughter, Henry. I'll let you know when I want to leave.'

'Yes, sir, Mr Novak.'

Callie had already gone back to her duties, and as Henry was about to follow her Joanna said, 'Perhaps you'd ask Rowena to bring us some iced tea? I'm sure Mr Novak is ready for a drink.'

'A beer would be better,' muttered Oliver, but both Joanna and Henry pretended not to hear him. It was too early in the day to start drinking alcohol.

After Henry had gone, Joanna seated herself on one of the chairs beside the bamboo table where she often did her work.

Then, with another smile for her visitor, she said, 'How are you? I know Matt's been worried about you.'

'Has he?' Oliver didn't sound as if he believed that, but he leant across to pat Joanna's arm with his right hand. 'More to the point, how are you? I couldn't believe my ears when Matt told me you were having a baby.'

Joanna felt a deepening of colour in her cheeks. 'I couldn't believe it either. Not at first,' she admitted honestly. 'After all those false alarms.'

'But you're pleased about it?'

'Oh, yes. I'm delighted.'

'Even though Matt's the father?'

Especially because Matt's the father, thought Joanna ruefully, but she kept that to herself.

'We're working things out,' she said instead, and Oliver regarded her with thoughtful eyes.

'I was sorry to hear about your father,' he said suddenly. 'Even though he was no friend of mine, I wouldn't have wished him ill.'

'Thank you.'

'But I have to say, he caused a lot of unhappiness for you and Matt, and I'm hoping that this baby will go some way to healing the wounds between you.'

Joanna sighed. 'Oh, Oliver—'

She would have said more, but Rowena arrived at that moment with a jug of iced tea.

In all honesty, Joanna was glad of the diversion. She had the feeling that Matt's father hadn't just come here to say hello. Pouring the iced tea gave her time to absorb what he was saying, but she was still not prepared for what was to come.

Setting his tea aside, Oliver regarded her intently. 'I know you and Matt are not back together,' he said quietly, 'but I'm here to tell you that your father was not the innocent he claimed to be.' He sighed. 'There were things Matt didn't tell you. Things he was fool enough to keep to himself. And then, when he did try to explain the situation, you wouldn't listen to him.'

Joanna shifted a little uncomfortably. 'Oliver—'

'No, listen to me.' It was obvious he felt strongly about what he was saying, but she was a little alarmed to see the colour that had entered his cheeks as he spoke. 'Your father resented me from the moment I married Matt's mother. He and Adrienne were sweethearts, you know? While she was at college in England.'

Joanna's jaw dropped. 'You know about that?'

'Ah.' Oliver nodded. 'I'm surprised he told you. In any case, it doesn't matter,' he went on firmly. 'He should have known that my father was every bit as astute as I believe I am, and there was nothing Adrienne did before our marriage that John Novak didn't know about.'

'I don't see what that has to do—'

'It has everything to do with his attitude towards Matt. Joanna, Angus knew his firm was in difficulties before you married my son, and to begin with it was enough for him to have Matt bail him out.'

'He was very grateful.'

'Was he?' Oliver's tone was ironic now. 'Well, I have to tell you, Jo, that gratitude didn't last very long.'

'If you're talking about the accident—'

'Of course, I'm talking about the accident.' Oliver reached for his glass and managed to take a mouthful of tea.

'It was unfortunate that Angus had been diagnosed with terminal cancer at the time, but that was no reason for him to tell lies about my son.'

Joanna shifted awkwardly. 'If they were lies,' she murmured unhappily, not wanting to start an argument. The baby was restless and talking about her father again was setting her nerves on edge.

But Oliver had evidently decided to speak his mind.

'Matt did everything he could to save Carlyle's reputation,' he said tersely. 'But the markings on the steel they'd used to build the platform spoke for themselves.'

Joanna bent her head. 'I suppose you would say that. Matt's your son.'

'Matt is an honest man, which is more than I can say for Angus Carlyle.' Joanna noticed Oliver was breathing quickly now, and she tried to change the subject by offering him more tea.

But Oliver wasn't finished. 'You didn't know about his gambling, did you, Jo?' He was evidently finding it difficult to speak now. 'My God, that man had a lot to answer for.'

Matt wasn't in the best of moods.

His mother and father had arrived a couple of days ago. And, although he'd been delighted to see that his father had made considerable progress with his mobility, his mother's attitude was beginning to get on his nerves.

She lost no opportunity to deplore Matt's decision to bring his ex-wife to the island, which was another reason for his sour disposition. Thankfully, his father didn't share her opinion, and this morning he'd had Henry take him to the cottage to see Joanna herself.

Matt had to wonder what his father would say to her.

When Oliver had heard that Joanna's father was blaming NovCo for the accident in the Alaskan oil field, he'd been furious. They all knew—including Angus—that the equipment they'd been using had been built in the Carlyle yard. But by the time Matt had got back from New York, Joanna had heard her father's version of the story. His claim, that NovCo was using his name to protect their own interests, had apparently seemed believable to her.

It had all been lies, of course. Matt had been stunned by Angus's betrayal. He'd spent those last weeks in New York trying to protect the old man's reputation. Angus had been dying, and the last thing Matt had wanted on his obituary was the revelation that he'd been cheating his own company.

Of course, Joanna hadn't believed him. Angus had never lied, she'd said, and she had no reason to think he was lying now. But the bitterest thing of all was when Angus had told Joanna that Matt had been keeping secrets from her, daring Matt to reveal Angus's addiction to his wife.

And, of course, he hadn't. What could he have said? Matt wondered now. Angus had wagered that Matt wouldn't chance deepening the rift between them by revealing her father's weaknesses, and when Joanna had demanded to know what her father was talking about, he'd had to deny any knowledge of it.

Angus had been a gambler to the last.

Matt scowled. It was all right to think that Joanna should have had more faith in him, but it was easy to be wise after the event. He feared he was wasting his time, hoping she would stay with him, despite what she'd said. If she hadn't believed him before, why should she believe him now?

He was in his office at present, trying desperately to complete an article, and when his mother burst into the room, he didn't know how he kept his temper.

'What?' he asked flatly. 'Ma, if this is—'

'You'd better come,' she interrupted him. 'Powell says that your father's not feeling well. I believe he's had an argument with Joanna and he's resting in one of the bedrooms at the cottage.'

Adrienne sniffed. 'Don't say I didn't warn you,' she said coldly, as Matt pushed past her onto the veranda. 'That woman has been nothing but trouble ever since you met her.'

In the event, Matt found his father sleeping, and, judging from his appearance, he had probably just over-tired himself. Joanna was hovering over him, looking anxious, but Oliver looked well enough.

'It was my fault,' she said unhappily. 'He was

talking about my father.' She licked her lips and looked up at her ex-husband. 'He—he told me Daddy was a gambler. Is that true?'

'Of course, it's true,' said Adrienne disparagingly, who had come into the room behind her son, but Matt hustled her and Joanna out of the bedroom so that they didn't disturb his father.

'Not now,' he said, dark eyes boring warningly into his mother's. He might regret this chance to redeem himself, but right now he was more concerned about Joanna. 'I've sent for Dr Rodrigues. He should be here soon.'

The doctor arrived soon after, by which point Matt had ensured that Joanna had had a drink and was comfortably installed in a chair on the veranda. He'd sent his mother back to the villa with Henry and couldn't help a sigh of relief when she'd gone.

He spoke to Dr Rodrigues privately, before the other man could get out of his car. Matt was actually more concerned about Joanna. He'd noticed how agitated she'd become.

The doctor looked in on Oliver first and, according to him, Matt's father was probably only exhausted, as Matt had thought. When Joanna had had her blood pressure taken, however, the medic looked anxious. He was of the opinion that she should rest completely for the next twenty-four hours.

Joanna stared at him. 'What do you mean? Rest completely? Are you saying I should stay in bed?'

'That would be best,' said Rodrigues, looking a little rueful. 'You were so well when I saw you a few weeks ago. What have you been doing to raise your blood pressure? This isn't the time to be indulging in marathons, you know?'

'I haven't.' Joanna glanced guiltily at Matt. 'I walk every day, but that's all.'

Matt's lips tightened. 'Is she ill?'

'No.' The doctor shook his head. 'But her blood pressure is higher than it ought to be at this stage of her pregnancy. We don't want to have to consider a condition called pre-eclampsia.'

Matt shook his head, his stomach muscles tightening apprehensively. 'I gather from your expression that it isn't a good condition.'

'No, it can be serious, but I'm not suggesting Mrs Novak is in danger. But she needs to rest and avoid any undue stimulation.'

Matt swallowed a little convulsively. 'But she will be okay?'

'She and the baby,' agreed Dr Rodrigues reassuringly. 'My wife is a midwife, as you possibly know. I'd like her to examine Mrs Novak, and perhaps she could stay here at Long Point for the next couple of days?'

'With pleasure,' said Matt eagerly. 'I suggest moving Joanna to the villa. We have more room there and I can keep an eye on her myself.'

Joanna caught her lower lip between her teeth. 'Is that necessary?' The last thing she wanted was to have to spend time with Adrienne.

'I think it is necessary,' declared Rodrigues. 'Don't worry, Mrs Novak. I have the suspicion that this baby won't be long in being born.'

'But I still have three weeks to go!' she protested.

'Dates can be wrong,' said Rodrigues solemnly. 'So, if that's all right with you, Mr Novak?'

'Of course.' Matt nodded, and, ignoring Joanna's silent protest, he took her hand. 'Relax, Jo. You can leave it with me.'

Joanna was installed in the bedroom she'd occupied on her first night at Long Point, after she'd been frightened by the hutia in the cottage. Matt knew she hadn't wanted to come here, particularly as his mother was still in residence, and, after her conversation with Oliver Novak, she would rather have avoided him, too.

The trouble was, she couldn't forget the things

he'd told her. Somehow, hearing Matt's father tell her that Angus Carlyle had been a gambler rang true. Oliver had no axe to grind; particularly not now. The court case was over and the compensation had been paid long ago.

All right, perhaps he was just defending his son. But, after reading that email on her father's laptop, Joanna couldn't help thinking that it all made sense.

Her father had never mentioned his previous relationship with Adrienne either. If she hadn't found that letter, she would never have suspected they'd had an affair. But it was a relief to know that Oliver knew about it. That was one secret she didn't have to keep.

Looking back now, she guessed that when she'd turned up in Miami, Matt must have thought she'd come to realise there were two sides to every argument. Instead of which, she'd still believed what her father had told her, instead of taking the word of the man she loved.

The man she loved!

Joanna caught her breath. Was that true? Had she ever stopped loving Matt? If only he would give her another chance, she thought despairingly. Dared she tell him she wished she'd never got the divorce?

Matt came to see her after supper. To her relief, no one else appeared. Except Elsa Rodrigues, the doctor's wife who was a midwife, and who had examined her thoroughly before pronouncing that she agreed with her husband: Joanna might have the baby a little earlier than she'd expected.

For his part, Matt thought he'd never seen Joanna look lovelier, the bloom of her pregnancy adding a becoming softness to her face. During the last week, every time he'd visited the cottage, he'd fought the desire to ask her what she really wanted from him. What he wanted from her was getting easier to explain.

He knew his mother would think he was crazy if he admitted he wanted Joanna back. But could he really believe that the rapport they'd found in recent weeks was just because of the baby?

Seating himself on the side of the bed, he regarded her closely. 'How are you feeling?' he asked. 'I noticed you didn't eat much for your supper.'

'I wasn't hungry,' Joanna admitted, allowing him to take her hand. 'I'm sorry if I've created a problem. I had no idea the doctor would send me to bed.'

'It's no problem,' said Matt gently. 'And my father and mother are going home tomorrow anyway. I'm just sorry if my father said anything to upset you. I should have suspected he had an ulterior motive when he asked Henry to take him to see you.'

'Well, I'm glad he came,' said Joanna staunchly. 'I had no idea—'

She broke off abruptly, pressing a hand to her stomach. A pain had just knifed through her abdomen, and although she'd had some backache since Matt had ferried her to the cottage in the SUV, this was something else.

'What's wrong?'

Matt was immediately aware of her discomfort. His eyes had darkened in alarm, and she was desperate to reassure him.

This was definitely not the time to give him a master class in Braxton Hicks.

'It was nothing,' she denied, arching her back a little to relieve the constriction. 'I'm always having little aches and pains. It's just that you're not usually around when they occur.'

'I'd like to be,' muttered Matt, his voice raw with emotion. 'I know you might not agree, but I wish you'd stay here until the baby is born.'

'I'd like that—' Joanna was beginning, when another pain attacked her abdomen. She struggled to breathe the way she'd been told, and then whispered faintly, 'I think that might be sooner than we think.'

Matt didn't hesitate. Opening the bedroom door, he yelled for Rowena to fetch Mrs Rodrigues from her room, and then pulled his mobile phone out of his pocket. 'I hope to hell Jacob isn't taking the evening off. If he is, I'll fly the bloody helicopter myself.'

'I don't think we have time to summon the helicopter,' declared Elsa Rodrigues, coming into the room before he could make the call. 'I have a feeling this baby is likely to arrive within the next couple of hours. If you have no objections, Matt, I think we should make preparations for the birth right here.'

Matt looked down at Joanna. 'Jo,' he said thickly, feeling guilty. 'I never meant for this to happen.'

'Nor me,' murmured Joanna faintly, and then broke off when another spasm gripped her. She looked up at him through tear-filled eyes. 'But stay with me, Matt? Please. Stay with me and hold my hand?'

CHAPTER TWENTY-ONE

MATT WAS SITTING on the veranda when Dr Rodrigues came to find him. He'd been trying to doze, but the events of the past ten hours had left him too full of adrenalin to rest. Now, sunlight was sparkling on the leaves of the palm trees and gilding the edge of the water with a pale translucent light.

'Joanna is awake,' the doctor said softly. His wife had sent for him as soon as she was confident that the baby's head had been engaged. Then with more assurance, he added, 'Your mother is with her.'

'My mother!'

Matt groaned, getting to his feet at once. What the hell was Adrienne doing there? He guessed she would be the last person Joanna wanted to see. His ex-wife had been exhausted when he'd left her four hours ago, and Matt had been grateful that Elsa had taken the baby away so that Joanna could sleep.

For his part, Matt was still digesting the news that he was a father. The baby's birth had happened so quickly. He'd always thought that first babies could take days and not hours to arrive, but he'd been wrong.

Joanna had been lucky. Her labour had been fairly arduous without any pain relief, but when they'd both gazed in wonder at the tiny baby boy who had come so precipitately into the world, everything else was forgotten.

Despite weighing more than eight pounds, he'd seemed so absurdly fragile. And for a few minutes, sitting beside Joanna on the bed, Matt had felt they were a real family at last.

Then Elsa had insisted on ushering him out of the room to allow Joanna to rest. He'd promised to return as soon as she was awake, but now it seemed his mother had beaten him to it. He couldn't help the suspicion that her visit was not a friendly one.

Walking across the marble-tiled foyer, Matt was shocked to hear raised voices coming from the bedroom where Joanna was resting. The loudest was his mother's, if he didn't miss his guess. Joanna's contribution much less aggressive. What the hell was going on?

Reaching the door, Matt was about to burst

into the room, when he was halted by Adrienne's next words.

'It's not your call,' Adrienne was saying angrily. 'Nothing you do is going to change Matt's mind.'

Joanna's response was spoken in a much quieter tone. 'I just think this is Matt's and my decision, not yours.'

'We'll see about that—' Adrienne was beginning threateningly, but Matt had heard enough.

Thrusting open the door, he halted on the threshold, the scene that met his eyes filling him with a mixture of pleasure and dread. There was no sign of Elsa, but she had evidently brought the baby because Joanna was holding him close to her chest. Adrienne, meanwhile, was leaning over her, as if she was about to snatch the baby out of her arms.

'In God's name, what's going on here?' Matt demanded, glaring at his mother. The atmosphere in the room was decidedly hostile and he couldn't understand why. 'Don't you think Joanna's had enough to cope with in the last twelve hours without you causing a scene?'

Adrienne immediately stepped back from the bed. With a forced smile, she said, 'Oh, Matt, I didn't see you there.' She paused to lick her lips. 'And you couldn't be more wrong. I don't want to cause a scene.' She gave the girl a tight-lipped glance. 'Joanna simply won't listen to reason.'

Joanna said nothing. She knew better than to try and argue with Matt's mother in this mood. Instead, she looked down at her baby son and wondered why she'd ever thought that Adrienne had come here to heal their differences.

Matt turned to Joanna, and when she still didn't try to defend herself, he looked again at his mother. 'I don't know what this is all about,' he said, 'but now is not the time to be upsetting *anyone.*'

'I didn't come here to upset her,' retorted Adrienne, taking a step away from the bed. 'But if you do intend to play some part in your son's life, Matt, you have to make a stand.'

Matt scowled. 'And this affects you how, exactly?'

'Well, I am the child's grandmother,' declared his mother shortly. 'If you allow Joanna to take your son back to England, you may never see him again.'

Matt sucked in a frustrated breath. 'The child's less than five hours old, Ma. We've got plenty of time to think about his future.'

Adrienne's lips tightened. 'Now you're being ridiculously naïve, Matt. I'm not suggesting you ask for custody of the infant straight away. All I'm saying is—'

'Dammit, you were casting doubts on the child's parentage a couple days ago,' Matt reminded her harshly. 'I suggest you go back to Dad, Mother. I'll let you know what's happening when Joanna and I have had time to talk.'

Joanna sighed, shifting the baby to a more comfortable position. Although she'd had a short nap, she was still absurdly tired. And weepy, too. Hearing Matt and his mother talk about her son as if she weren't even present made her feel invisible.

But one thing was certain: No one was going to take him away from her.

'Anyway, we'll talk later,' Matt was saying now, and Joanna saw the way Adrienne cast an angry look in her direction.

Does she think I might tell Matt about her affair with my father? Joanna wondered incredulously. Just because Oliver was aware of her affair, didn't mean he'd told her.

Joanna almost felt sorry for her. For all her bluster, Adrienne was as vulnerable as anybody else. But she seemed determined that Matt should have custody of the baby, and Joanna knew the Novaks had the money to employ lawyers to override any argument she might make.

Now Adrienne headed with evident reluctance for the door. 'You'll let me know what you decide, won't you, darling?' she said, with another hostile look in Joanna's direction. 'Your father and I just want to do what's best for you, you know?'

As she was about to depart, Elsa appeared. 'I'm sorry to intrude,' she began. 'Is everything all right here? The baby—'

'The baby's fine,' said Matt, approaching the bed. 'Will you let Elsa take him for a while, Jo? I'm worried about you. You look exhausted.'

Joanna gazed across at Elsa with tears in her eyes. 'Don't let Matt's mother take my baby away, will you?' she begged. 'He's all I've got.'

'You've got me,' exclaimed Matt, uncaring what his mother thought now. He sat down on the side of the bed and cupped Joanna's face between his hands. 'And nobody's going to do anything without your say-so.' He paused. 'But perhaps you should let Elsa take him for a while.'

'I can look after him,' said Adrienne at once, but Matt gave her a warning look.

'Not now,' he said forcefully. 'I think you've done enough.'

'I was only thinking of you, Matt,' she protested, but Matt ignored her.

'Just go,' he said. 'You've got packing to do.'

'Matt!'

Her voice was loud with protest and Dr Rodrigues, who had appeared behind his wife, came into the room.

'I can hear your voices in the study, Mr Novak. I told you, Joanna needs to rest.'

Matt sighed. 'I know. And I'm sorry.'

'Yes, well, whatever it is you need to say to one another, surely it can wait until Joanna is stronger?'

Now Matt took charge. 'You were just leaving, weren't you, Ma?' he said, looking at his mother, and Adrienne was not prepared to say any more in front of the doctor and his wife.

To Joanna's relief, Matt saw them all out of the door and closed it. Then he turned back to the bed. 'I'm sorry about that,' he said huskily, resuming his seat beside her. He stroked her cheek with gentle fingers. 'I'm sorry for a lot of things. I never meant for you to discover the truth about your dad. And the timing couldn't have been worse!'

Joanna lifted a hand to cover his, looking up at him with anxious eyes. 'But it is true, isn't it? He had a gambling addiction, didn't he?' she whispered. 'It explains so much.'

'Yeah, well, the old man made me promise not

to tell you.' Suddenly Matt didn't want to talk about it anymore. 'Do you believe me now, Jo?'

Joanna sniffed. 'Matt, ever since I came to the island, I've found myself wanting to put the past behind me. You must know that. I haven't exactly pushed you away.'

'I hoped that was so. But I was afraid I was getting the wrong message,' said Matt huskily. 'When something means so much to you, you tend not to believe it.'

Joanna squeezed his hand. 'I've been such a fool. Can you ever forgive me?'

'We've both been fools.' Matt groaned. 'Why the hell do you think I wanted you here? I wanted to take care of you. I wanted us to be together. I—hoped you might want to stay.'

Joanna met his eyes. 'I do want to stay,' she said eagerly. 'I never thought I'd say that when you insisted on me coming here, but I do.'

Matt shook his head. 'When I left your apartment in London, I was convinced that was the end of us.'

Joanna nodded. 'So was I.'

He grimaced. 'That's not to say I wouldn't have tried again. You know I love you. I never stopped loving you, no matter what garbage came out of my mouth at the time.'

'Do you mean that?' Joanna caught her breath, looking up at him through tear-drenched lashes. 'You love me?'

'Of course, I love you,' he muttered thickly, raising her hand to his lips. His tongue brushed her knuckles with the utmost tenderness. 'I want us to be married again. I never want to let you go.'

'Oh, Matt, I love you, too.' There was so much more she wanted to say to him, but it could wait. 'I was so stupid to let anyone come between us.'

'Hey, he was your father,' said Matt gently. 'I just kept on hoping that sooner or later the truth would come out.'

'Will you forgive me for doubting you? If I promise to spend the rest of my life making amends?'

'I may keep you to that,' said Matt, looping one hand at her nape and pulling her towards him. Then, after kissing her until she was breathless, he added, 'I just wanted to hear you say you love me. That's all I ever wanted. And to be with you and our son.'

'I'm so glad you were there at his birth. When he's older, you'll be able to tell him so.'

'*We'll* be able to tell him so,' Matt amended with some satisfaction, before kissing his wife again.

EPILOGUE

A WEEK LATER Joanna wheeled the baby down the path to the jetty.

Matt had gone out in his dinghy earlier that morning for the first time since the baby was born. He hadn't wanted to leave her, but Joanna had insisted she could manage on her own. Well, with Callie's help, she appended. Teresa and Henry's granddaughter had proved her weight in gold since the baby's birth.

Adrienne and Oliver had gone home the day after the baby's birth, and Oliver seemed satisfied that he had played some part in Joanna's and Matt's reunion.

For her part, Joanna knew that she and Adrienne would never be friends. But Matt's mother had apparently accepted that, as they were getting married again, there was no point in depriving herself of her grandson by trying to keep them apart.

Jealousy was a terrible thing, and Joanna guessed Adrienne would have been jealous of any woman who took her son away from her. Discovering Joanna was Angus Carlyle's daughter must have been doubly distressing. Particularly when her husband had announced he was going into business with her old lover. She must have lived in fear of their previous relationship being made public.

Joanna wondered now if Angus had sought to destroy her and Matt's marriage to hurt Adrienne. As with so much else, his actions were hard to forgive.

To be charitable, Joanna knew her father's illness had changed him. Learning he was suffering from terminal cancer had made him brooding and resentful of other people's happiness. Even her own.

But that was in the past. Matt and Joanna were planning to get married again as soon as they could. And then, later, they'd agreed to return to Miami for the baby's christening.

Joanna had destroyed Adrienne's letter. That was one piece of poison that would never again see the light of day. She and Matt were together and that was all that mattered. She really hoped that her father had forgotten the letter was there.

She could feel the sun's rays on her shoulders as she emerged from the shadow of the palms, but she didn't mind. It was so good to be out and about again, so good to be able to wear an outfit that didn't outline the swollen curve of her stomach.

Their son lay on his back in the stroller, protected by the shade cast by its hood. Matt had had the baby carriage flown over from Nassau the same day the baby was born. Along with baby clothes and equipment of every kind.

It was a thrilling time for Joanna. And Matt, too, she knew. Their son was a constant delight to both of them but, more importantly, they were rediscovering every aspect of their love for one another.

Joanna heard Henry's voice and a moment later she saw her husband vaulting onto the jetty. He hadn't been out very long, she thought humorously. Evidently, since he'd become a father, sailing had lost much of its appeal.

Matt saw Joanna at once, and, leaving Henry to moor the craft, he came striding towards her. 'I've missed you,' he said huskily, slipping his arm about her shoulders, uncaring who was watching them. He bent his head and covered her lips with his. Then, with some concern, 'Should you be out in this heat?'

'Well, if I'm going to live here, I've got to get

used to it,' replied Joanna, slipping her arm about his waist. 'We are going to live here, aren't we?'

'I like the way you say "we",' murmured Matt, his eyes devouring her. 'How did I ever live without you?'

Matt bent to bury his face in the curve of her shoulder and Joanna cupped his neck with gentle fingers. 'I should have believed you all along.'

Matt lifted his head. 'Yeah, you should,' he agreed roughly. 'I've never lied to you, and I never will.'

Joanna gnawed on her lower lip. 'Will you believe me if I tell you that soon after I got here, I was prepared to put all that behind us and ask you if I could stay?'

'Because of the baby?'

'No, because of us,' exclaimed Joanna huskily. 'I didn't want you to think I had any ulterior motive for being here, but perhaps I had.'

Matt stared at her. 'Do you mean that?'

'Of course, I mean it.' She paused. 'But after—after that—that time on the beach, you seemed so—remote.'

'I wanted to see you; of course, I did.' Matt groaned. 'But it was hard to know what I was going to say. Then my parents being there meant we couldn't have a private conversation.' He paused. 'But surely it was obvious how I felt? I couldn't keep my hands off you.'

There was another satisfying moment, and then Henry's hearty voice broke into their embrace. 'Would you like me to take your son back to the villa?' he asked, peering into the stroller and making goo-goo noises at the baby.

Matt grinned at Joanna. 'I didn't know you were a nursemaid, Henry,' he said, and the older man lifted his head to pull a face.

'I thought you might like a little privacy, that's all,' he said innocently. 'Particularly with Mrs Sophie coming this afternoon.'

'God, I'd forgotten that. She's dying to see her nephew, I know.' Then Matt looked at Joanna. 'So, what do you think? Have you got time to take a walk along the beach with me?'

'A walk?' she echoed, handing the stroller into Henry's capable hands. 'Why, Mr Novak, I do believe I have. Do you mind if I take your arm?'

'I'm hoping you'll take every part of me,' murmured Matt in an undertone, and Joanna was still giggling when Henry disappeared from view.

* * * * *

MILLS & BOON®
Large Print – December 2017

"An Heir Made in the Marriage Bed "
Anne Mather EQBS 2018

The Prince's Stolen Virgin
Maisey Yates

Protecting His Defiant Innocent
Michelle Smart

Pregnant at Acosta's Demand
Maya Blake

The Secret He Must Claim
Chantelle Shaw

Carrying the Spaniard's Child
Jennie Lucas

A Ring for the Greek's Baby
Melanie Milburne

The Runaway Bride and the Billionaire
Kate Hardy

The Boss's Fake Fiancée
Susan Meier

The Millionaire's Redemption
Therese Beharrie

Captivated by the Enigmatic Tycoon
Bella Bucannon

MILLS & BOON®
Large Print – January 2018

The Tycoon's Outrageous Proposal
Miranda Lee

Cipriani's Innocent Captive
Cathy Williams

Claiming His One-Night Baby
Michelle Smart

At the Ruthless Billionaire's Command
Carole Mortimer

Engaged for Her Enemy's Heir
Kate Hewitt

His Drakon Runaway Bride
Tara Pammi

The Throne He Must Take
Chantelle Shaw

A Proposal from the Crown Prince
Jessica Gilmore

Sarah and the Secret Sheikh
Michelle Douglas

Conveniently Engaged to the Boss
Ellie Darkins

Her New York Billionaire
Andrea Bolter

MILLS & BOON®

Why shop at millsandboon.co.uk?

Each year, thousands of romance readers find their perfect read at millsandboon.co.uk. That's because we're passionate about bringing you the very best romantic fiction. Here are some of the advantages of shopping at www.millsandboon.co.uk:

* **Get new books first**—you'll be able to buy your favourite books one month before they hit the shops

* **Get exclusive discounts**—you'll also be able to buy our specially created monthly collections, with up to 50% off the RRP

* **Find your favourite authors**—latest news, interviews and new releases for all your favourite authors and series on our website, plus ideas for what to try next

* **Join in**—once you've bought your favourite books, don't forget to register with us to rate, review and join in the discussions

Visit **www.millsandboon.co.uk**
for all this and more today!